In a Deep, Dark December

five festive chillers

by **Paul Finch**

Top Ten Sunday Times bestselling crime and horror author

Cover art by Neil Williams

https://paulfinch-writer.blogspot.com/

CONTENTS

The Christmas Toys – 1

Midnight Service – 23

The Faerie – 42

The Mummers – 70

The Killing Ground – 101

THE CHRISTMAS TOYS

Spazzer met Tookey inside the north gate of the park.

They hung back to ensure they wouldn't be seen by traffic passing on the road, though scarfed and capped as they were on this snowy Christmas Eve, it was unlikely anyone would be able to identify them. They watched the house directly opposite. It was set back behind its own front garden, and concealed from the road by a two-deep row of privets, but it was brightly lit as so many houses were at this time of year: alternating blue and yellow tubes of fairy lights were woven along its eaves; three glowing angels – white gowned cherubs with swans' wings – held a static procession on the apex of the roof. Tookey eyed them uneasily as he stood in the shadows of the park.

"This part of town's pretty well protected," he said. "Cased the place properly?"

"Been watching it for two weeks," Spazzer replied. "Deffo no alarm."

"None that we can see."

Spazzer chuckled. "You think they've got a direct line to the cop shop? It's a bit posh, but that's all. Hardly Millionaire's Row."

"So why we doing it?"

"'Cos it'll be a piece of piss. Family goes out every night around seven. I followed 'em yesterday. They're rehearsing for a charity concert at St. Aiden's. Performance is tonight, so there's no chance of them coming back early."

So they were church people, Tookey thought, discomforted. And St. Aiden's? – that was on one of the sink estates down in town. Not only were they church people, then, they were church people trying to raise money for good causes.

"But guess what, it gets better!" Spazzer was tall but rail-thin. His tattooed face narrowed, and he smiled a ferrety smile. "It's just as well hidden by trees at the back and sides. Once we're on the plot no one will be able to see us. So no alarm and we can take our time. How about it? Ripe for the plucking, or what?"

Tookey was shorter and dumpier than Spazzer, with pale, snail-like features and greasy, carrot-red hair, a messy fringe of which stuck out around the edges of his woolly cap. At a glance, he was no less odious-looking than his accomplice, and he'd clocked up at least as much jail time, but on this occasion he simply wasn't happy.

"Okay, it's an easy break," he said. "But if it's not Millionaire's Row, what's the point?"

"I had a gander through the lounge window," Spazzer replied. "You've never seen as many prezzies."

"We're here to pinch Christmas presents?"

"There must be three hundred of 'em. And in this kind of neighbourhood it'll be top-end stuff. I bet there's five grand's worth there, easy."

"Who lives here, Spaz?"

Spazzer scratched at the wart on his lip. "Weird looking bunch, if you want my opinion. Bloke's tall, got a load of grey hair like a feather duster. Wife's younger, forties maybe, dark hair. Great tits and arse."

"So it's just a couple of adults?" Tookey sounded hopeful.

"Nah, there's two kids as well. Boy and a girl. Always screaming and running around when they're going out to the car, chucking snowballs and that."

"You won't feel a bit shitty … pinching the kiddies' presents on Christmas Eve?"

Spazzer shrugged. "Everything'll be covered by insurance."

"They'll have a job getting anything out of the insurance if there's no alarm."

"Their fault, isn't it? Look Took, these swanky bastards, it's not like they can't afford to buy more stuff."

Tookey glanced back at the house. It looked charmingly festive: snow coating its roof and the encircling fir trees; icicles hanging over its windows, lamplight spilling warmly from the diamond-paned side-panel next to the front door. "Seems wrong, that's all."

"Wrong? Are you going soft?" Now that his plan was being criticised, there was a harsher edge to Spazzer's voice. With his lanky, emaciated physique, he was no physical menace. But he was connected; he only needed to put the word out that Tookey was becoming unreliable and the work would dry up.

"It's just that Christmas spirit thing, I suppose," Tookey said.

"Christmas what?"

"Spirit … I'm sure you've heard of it."

"I've got an idea, Took … why don't you shut your gob and let me do the worrying."

"Whatever."

"You've brought the van?"

"End of Miry Lane, like you said."

"Canvas?"

"Covered. The way this snow's coming down it'll look like it's been there hours."

Spazzer felt under his jacket. A crackle of plastic denoted the wrapping on his tool kit. "In that case … let's do it."

*

It was close on nine o'clock in the evening and only the odd taxi trundled by. The snow was still falling, an ice-edged wind driving the flakes diagonally. Everything – the park's paths and lawns, the pavements on either side of the road – was covered to a depth of maybe seven inches. Spazzer and Tookey walked straight across from the park gate, hands in pockets, heads bowed. They would only be exposed on the open road for about five seconds, which was a risk, though less so than normal. If anyone spotted them now all they'd observe were two vague figures muffled by the feathery deluge. At the top of the drive, in addition to the garish neon adorning the roof, a motion-sensitive light shone from over the garage door. The blizzard had triggered this long before they'd arrived, and would ensure it remained activated. But as Spazzer had said, the trees along the side and around the back of the house were so tall and dense that the property was well concealed. They sidled into the narrow passage between the house and the garage. Here Spazzer halted, fumbling under his jacket for his kit.

"How do we get in?" Tookey whispered.

Spazzer tapped on a side-window, before inserting his chisel next to its jamb and waggling it into place. "This opens direct into the hall."

Tookey glanced cautiously around. At the far end of the side passage, a second motion-sensitive light illuminated the rear garden. From the narrow sliver Tookey could see of it, its expansive lawn was a wilderness of white, with a black meshwork of leafless branches marking its perimeter. Thinking he'd heard something down there, he peered more closely, straining his vision to focus through the billowing flakes, but seeing nothing. Spazzer meanwhile began tapping his chisel with his rag-wrapped mallet. Again, Tookey thought he heard something at the end of the passage – and this time he saw it.

An enormous shape had bounced into view.

He almost shouted. He probably would have had Spazzer not clamped a gloved hand to his mouth. They stared in wordless disbelief at what looked to be a gigantic, rubbery animal bobbing about at the end of the side passage. Its outline initially flummoxed them because it was completely white in colour. But then they saw its massive, raised arms complete with genuine curved claws, and a wide-open, bright red mouth. "Polar bear?" Tookey said in a whisper. "Fucking polar bear!" The object, which was at least seven feet tall, blocked the entire end of the passage, but still bobbed from side to side as if shifting with the eddies of snow. "Tell me that's inflatable."

"Course it's inflatable!" Spazzer hissed. "You didn't think it was real?"

"What the … what the hell is it …?"

"One of those daft blow-up decorations!"

"You knew it was here?"

"I saw it while I was poking around the other night. It wasn't inflated at the time."

"So why's it … why's it just suddenly …?"

“What does it matter?” Spazzer shrugged and snickered at his mate’s credulity. “They’re attached to pipes, aren’t they? And there are little motors running, and every so often they get filled with air and stand up. You must have seen them at footy grounds.”

Despite this sensible explanation, the object tilted forward as the snowflakes swirled behind it, as if it was attempting to force its way towards them along the passage.

“Stand back,” Spazzer said, returning his attention to the window.

It opened easily. There was minimal damage to its wooden frame and none whatever to the glass. Once inside they pulled the window closed and fitted it gently into place. Spazzer re-wrapped his tools, and slid them back into one of the many compartments inside his jacket. They now found themselves in an under-stair cubby hole adjoined to the hall. Compared to the exterior of the house, the interior was luxuriously warm. It also had the atmosphere of a woodland grove thanks to an eerie greenish light flooding through it. When they poked their heads out, they saw the reason for this: the entire hall had been richly decked with evergreens: great swags, bristling with frost-fringed pinecones, looped along its walls; holly, studded with crimson berries, wreathed every picture. Overhead hung an interwoven lattice of ivy and firs, above which innumerable fairy lights, all in varying shades of green, flickered gently.

“Santa’s grotto?” Spazzer snickered again.

At the end of the hall, near the internal front door, a slender but very tall imitation Christmas tree, twelve foot at least, had been erected. It was only possible for it to stand in this position because of the stairwell directly overhead. It was draped with streaks of white tinsel and hung with fragile blue and gold ornaments, and had a narrow, red-painted ladder propped up alongside it. Three other doorways opened off the hall. The one closest to the front presumably led to the lounge, the second probably connected with the dining room, and the third, the one at the rear of the building, looked like the entrance to the kitchen; bunches of evergreens, woven with ribbons and the scarlet blooms of poinsettias, had been placed artistically around the inside of its frame, creating a Yuletide arch.

For no particular reason, they padded through into the kitchen first. Its floor was of varnished brick, its fixtures and fittings of scrubbed pine. The only light in there came from the oven, in which a tray of mince pies was browning nicely. Other festive goodies covered the worktops: plates piled with sandwiches and canapés, mushroom vol-au-vents, chicken drumsticks, rolls of cold meat, sausages wrapped in bacon, prawns on skewers, pies, plum tarts and macaroons. The air was scented with orange and nutmeg; they traced the source of this to a pan on the stove containing a simmering purple fluid filled with leaves and chunks of fruit. A twist of mistletoe hung from the copper hood overhead.

"Planning quite a party," Spazzer said. He lifted a mug from a hook, dipped it in the mulled wine and took a sip. He rolled it around the inside of his mouth, a faux expert, before spitting it on the floor. He turned next to the food, thrusting handfuls into his mouth. "Might as well load up, Took … best nosh *we're* going to get this Christmas."

Tookey resisted. Though they allegedly had all night here, he was feeling increasingly nervous. Spazzer stripped the meat from a couple more chicken drumsticks, dropping the bones and gristle, and carefully licked the grease from the dirty, knitted fingers of his gloves – at which point they both jerked around, startled.

A low, electronic hum, with a repeating *click* at the centre of it, had commenced somewhere down at the other end of the hall. Tookey flattened himself out of sight while Spazzer risked a glance down the green-lit passage. There was no movement that he could discern, except suddenly … he chuckled loudly.

Tookey followed him along the hall. When they reached the tall Christmas tree, a diminutive figure was laboriously descending the red-painted ladder. It was a pint-sized Santa, complete with crimson cloak and hood and a sack on its back with a tiny candy cane poking out. The figure, which was no more than half a foot high, moved with a slow, clockwork stiffness.

"Tatty as fuck," Spazzer scoffed. "What are posh gits coming to, eh?" He licked his mittened fingers one more time, savouring every last speck of chicken grease, and then turned and went into the lounge.

This room was perhaps as large as the entire downstairs of the terraced house where Tookey lived with his father. Its carpet and furniture were deep and lush, and it had ornamental oak beams across its ceiling. It also had a huge granite fireplace, in the centre of which a pair of life-size costumed legs – in red trousers and black boots, trimmed with fur – had descended from the chimney and stood on top of a yule log swathed in green and silver ribbons. Festive cards were arranged neatly on all the walls. Masses of holly and ivy were bundled along the mantelpiece. Another large Christmas tree, not as tall as the first but more extravagantly clad, occupied one of the corners and was buried to a quarter of its depth in a chaotic heap of brightly coloured packages.

"Jesus," Tookey muttered. "We'll never shift all this."

“Told you.” Spazzer grabbed a roll of bin liners from his pocket, handing a couple to Tookey and keeping a couple for himself. “But you’re right, we can’t take it all. We can’t be going back and forward across the road all evening, so it’s two sacks each, max. Main thing is make sure you get all the heavy ones. That’ll be the good stuff.” He hunkered down, working his way on hands and knees through the great heap of presents, checking each one for size and weight.

Tookey again glanced around the room. Low-key lamplight enhanced its seasonal atmosphere. A fake but realistic candle burned at either end of the mantelpiece. There were Christmas figurines everywhere. Victorian carol singers on the bookshelves. On the floor to either side of the fireplace two pantomime soldiers in plumed tricornes and eighteenth century uniforms; their porcelain faces had been painted in bright dabs – sugarplum fairies on sentry duty. The lounge bay window gave out onto the front garden. Arrayed along its sill there was a snowman jazz band, each figure about a foot tall, all with the usual carrot noses and brass button eyes, but also wearing boaters and striped blazers; one carried a banjo, another a saxophone, while the third was seated behind a drum kit. It was true, Tookey reflected. Anyone who could afford all this could afford to miss out on a few presents.

“Tookey, move your arse, yeah!” Spazzer said. Tookey made to go over and join him, but glanced first at the snowman jazz band, all of whose heads were turned towards him. He felt certain they hadn’t been that way a minute ago.

“Tookey!”

“Okay, okay!” Tookey hunkered down. The more packages he bagged, all garnished with bows and tags and festive stamps, the easier it was to remind himself that he had never, either as child or adult, received such a torrent of gifts or even so many good wishes at Christmas time.

Spazzer had already filled his first sack and had lugged it out into the hall. Tookey now did the same with his, dumping it next to the internal front door – only to stop and glance around. Alongside him the mechanical Santa had halted midway down its ladder. Tookey found himself staring directly into its face, because apparently – and surely this was ridiculous – it had turned its head and looked at him. Briefly he was almost hypnotized. The tiny plastic face had blue pinpoints for eyes, but a sharp nose and its white beard jutted downward from its chin in demonic fashion. Tookey jumped when it abruptly hummed back to life, and recommenced its ungainly descent, its head swivelling back to the front.

"Spaz," he said, backing into the lounge, only to almost leap from his skin as the snowman jazz band came to life behind him.

... I wish it could be Christmas every daa-aa-aay! ...

Tookey spun around. The three figurines gyrated as they performed; the words and music blasting from some hidden speaker. As abruptly as it started, the caterwaul ceased, the snowmen all now facing different directions.

Spazzer had sat sharply upright. "Fuck's sake, what did you do?"

"Nothing, it just went off! And that Santa on the ladder …?"

"Be on timers, won't they? That shit's all the rage. Anyway, come on."

Tookey was about to cross the room, when he happened to glance at the doorway and saw the diminutive Santa figure standing there, still with a sack on its back, but now with head crooked around as if gazing into the lounge. "Fuck!" he shouted. The tiny shape was motionless, but it had clearly clambered off the ladder and crossed the hall under its own steam. "Is this thing supposed to walk around?"

"What?" Spazzer said, approaching.

"This thing … look!"

"What if it is?" Spazzer swung his foot, catapulting the tiny figure back into the hall, where there was a loud, shattering impact. "See … problem solved."

Tookey glanced uneasily at the other decorations.

"You know, Took," Spazzer said, "I reckon we've found a gold mine, here."

Tookey was still preoccupied. Why were the carol singers on the bookshelf looking at him? He was sure they'd been looking at each other before? "Eh?"

"No one's coming for another two hours. We've got the van just round the corner. Christ, we can clean this place out. I mean literally take *everything*."

Tookey finally realised what was being suggested. He glanced again at the mountain of presents. Two sacks were already full, and yet they'd barely made an impression on it. How long would it take to shift the rest? How many journeys to and from the van? How long would they have to remain in this house?

"Let's check the dining room," Spazzer said. "See if there's any silver."

Tookey protested as he followed him through. "What's silver worth these days?"

"I know someone who can move it. We'll get a tidy bit, don't fret."

Like the lounge, the dining room had oak beams along its ceiling, all looped with tendrils of ivy. A long dining table was laid out with cutlery, napkins and crêpe-wrapped crackers. Against one wall there was a mahogany sideboard with three Christmas trees arrayed on its polished surface. These were also imitations, mounted in beribboned buckets from the rear of which wires trailed across the sideboard. The tips of their branches were aglow with patterns of rippling colour.

"This it?" Tookey asked, picking up a fork.

"Nah." Spazzer yanked open a sideboard drawer. "Bunch of posh nobs like this … they'll have a decent service which they keep for best, not for family."

Hark, the herald angels siii-iiing ...

Three musical voices blasted out at high volume.

"Jesus Christ!" Even Spazzer jumped on this occasion.

Bewilderingly, three mouths had appeared, one in the foliage of each Christmas tree, though the joyous carol was clearly emitting from their buckets. Spazzer swiped one of the trees from the sideboard. As it crashed to the floor the carol abruptly halted. The tree's cables pulled taut, and the other trees followed it. "Can't stand cheap gimmicks!" he ranted, stomping and kicking, breaking branches, sending buckets spinning across the room, shedding circuitry

"Perhaps we'd better just split?" Tookey said.

"Not yet!" Spazzer retorted, yanking out more drawers.

Tookey glanced around. The dining room's window looked onto the rear garden, which was still dancing with flakes. It made an atmospheric backdrop for a generic but very detailed crib scene, which had been laid out on the windowsill. In fact, as he bent down to look, he realised that it was more than a crib; it appeared to be an entire representation of Bethlehem in miniature. Fleetingly, Tookey was touched by long ago memories of his infant school days, when the hopes and fears of all the years had seemed to apply to him as much as all the other kids. The flat-roofed houses were brown or beige, as if moulded from mud-brick, the glow of mellow lamplight visible from each interior, donkeys and camels yoked outside. In the very centre, on a raised mound, there was a stable, its frontage removed, revealing a baby in a manger and toy soldier-sized figures of Mary and Joseph kneeling one to either side. Above them, a single star was suspended. Somewhere on the floor one of the wires to the fallen Christmas trees sparked, and the star began to shine with a pale, silvery luminescence. At the same time figures started moving in the town. Tookey watched in fascination as three or four men, again no more than toy soldier size but distinctly sinister in hoods and cloaks, and with curved daggers, roved up and down the narrow streets, moving along electric runners that he hadn't noticed previously. One by one they visited each house, the internal light to which would then turn blood-red – to the accompaniment of tinny shrieks.

"What the …?" Tookey breathed. He had some vague memory of a school lesson during which he'd been told about that bad-tempered bastard – wasn't his name 'Herod'? – having all the babies killed to try and get to Jesus. But Christ, you didn't put something like that in a Christmas decoration! "Spaz!" he said. "Spaz …"

"What?" Spazzer snapped, still yanking drawers from the sideboard.

Before Tookey could elaborate, he lurched backward – a massive figure had ballooned into the window in front of him. It was white and maybe seven feet tall. Its yawning scarlet mouth and plastic-tipped claws rapped on the glass. *"Jesus!"* he yelped.

Spazzer spun around, only to relax again on sight of the inflatable. "Fucking idiot … scared the crap out of me!"

The polar bear's claws continued rapping on the glass. Up close, its eyes were black, deep-set orbs; its jowls furrowed horrifically as they snarled back from realistic teeth. Tookey backed away until he collided with the dining table. He struck it so hard that cutlery fell. "I'm out of here, Spazzer. I'm telling you, mate, I'm out of here!"

"We're both out of here," Spazzer replied, giving up on the sideboard and kicking at it brutally, splintering one of its finely finished panels – the inflatable seemed to rap on the window all the louder. "Let's just take the presents and leg it."

They ducked back down the hall. The internal front door was locked, but there was a key to it on a shelf. On the other side lay a small porch, though two life-size wickerwork reindeer stood one to either side of it. They were spangled with brilliant white Christmas lights, but also tangled with wires, which, rather absurdly, stretched across the porch between them, forming a kind of barricade.

"Sort that lot out," Spazzer said. "I'll just check the bedrooms."

While Spazzer's feet clumped upstairs, Tookey attempted to drag the two reindeer into the hall, but immediately ran into problems. The wires connecting them to the mains were not only tangled, but appeared to pass under the felt floor tiles. After he'd torn a few of these up, he saw that the wires had been threaded through a hole drilled in the step between the porch and hall, which meant they also ran under the hall carpet, though one errant strand followed the woodwork of the doorjamb up towards the verdure-clad ceiling. When one of these cables fizzled and spat as he tugged on it, Tookey tried to find a junction box so that he could turn the power off, but there was no sign of any such thing, and the more he fiddled and twisted around, the more woven his feet became in the string of lights.

"Shit!" he hissed, tripping backward into the hall.

When he'd disentangled himself, the reindeer were still in the porch, now lying on top of each other, fairy-lit cables wreathed around them. A slight movement caught his eye. Through the festive archway, he saw a great white object pressed against the glass of the kitchen window. The blizzard must have driven the inflatable bear back along the rear of the house, yet even as he stared it became static – as if it was peering straight at him.

"What now?" Spazzer said, coming back downstairs.

"Nothing, I ..." Tookey broke away from the brief trance he'd been caught in, but made a double take at the kitchen window when he saw that it was empty again. "Anything up there?"

Spazzer showed him a cupped palm, in which a few meagre items of jewellery glittered. He shoved it into his pocket. "It's not a lot, but it's better than nothing. Great job, by the way." He indicated the two reindeer still blocking the porch.

"They're all tangled up with the lights. I tried to shift them but I couldn't."

Without a word, Spazzer jumped onto both objects with his feet, stomping and hacking, until they were little more than piles of splinters and cable. He now had no problem dragging them into the hall and dumping them to one side. "Next time I need your van, Tookey, I'll just take it and leave you at home." He opened the front door and peeked outside. "Fill a couple more sacks and follow me." He slung the first two sacks over his shoulder, but their combined weight almost toppled him backward. "Christ in a cartoon!" Tookey tried to help, but Spazzer shrugged him away. "Never mind me! Just get some more stuff!" Without looking back, Spazzer tottered outside, swaying out of sight down the drive. There was another wild jangle of Christmas jazz.

... Mary's boy-child, Jesus Christ, was born on ...

Tookey turned sharply. As he did, his feet again tangled in twists of fairy-lit cable. He staggered sideways against the Christmas tree. When he'd unravelled himself this second time, the music had ceased. He moved warily back into the lounge. All the jazz players' heads were turned in his direction. His eyes roved elsewhere around the room. Again, every figurine seemed to be watching him, their heads turned, even the sugarplum soldiers, which surely weren't even comprised of movable parts. He darted for the remaining bin liners, cramming parcels into the first one he got hold of, but overstuffing it so that when he tried to haul it across the room it ripped, and everything fell out. Time was no longer on his side, he realised in panic. But he couldn't leave this treasure trove empty-handed. He went for another sack, threw a few items inside and lugged it through into the hall, where snowflakes were gushing in through the wide open front door. For some reason this made him glance down the hall and through the kitchen window. That the polar bear was no longer there was hardly a problem – the wind was blowing the wretched thing all over the place. But then he heard a noise from the side of the house: a scraping and squeaking, as if some vast, inflatable form was forcing itself along the narrow passage towards the front.

Tookey charged at the front door, banging it closed. He backed away, regarding the flurrying flakes through the diamond-paned window, expecting some enormous shape to suddenly appear there. He was vaguely aware that he could hear the cries of babes as they died under chopping blades. Then he became aware of something else: a bumping, slithering sound. He glanced at the lounge door, not needing to go in there to know what he was hearing: those legs in the fireplace, the ones in black boots and red trim; he pictured them shifting about as they tried to release the great body from the chimney above. He pictured a gross, ungainly form, life-size of course, but black with soot as it slowly eased itself down. Maybe a pair of gloves were even now grasping the underside of the mantelpiece to provide leverage?

Tookey fled down the hall, thinking that if he could get out through the kitchen window, he could escape into a neighbouring garden. But en route his feet again tangled in loops of fairy lights and meshed fragments of wickerwork. There was an explosion of plaster as cables were yanked down from overhead. Swags of foliage fell too, the network of green lights above them following, all landing on Tookey in a single enveloping mass. It was so heavy that it almost knocked him to his knees. From all sides he was spiked by pine needles and the prickly edges of holly leaves. He pivoted around trying to free himself, but only knotting himself more tightly into the package. There were flashes as strings of lights began shorting and sparking. A live cable fell spitting across his shoulder. Another leapt around his feet like a snake. Tookey froze, sensing the damaged electricals all around him, but it was too little too late – as the heavy footsteps proceeding across the lounge would soon bear out.

*

Bowed beneath the weight of his two sacks, Spazzer stumbled along the meandering path that circled the edge of the park. He wasn't likely to meet anyone taking this little-used route, but it was still difficult, the deep, crisp snow causing him to trip and stagger. Miry Lane, which had seemed so convenient when he'd first planned this job, now felt a ridiculous distance away when they had so much gear to transport. One alternative would have been putting the van on the actual drive of the house, but suppose the family had come home early and blocked them in? Even if Tookey and Spazzer had managed to get away over the neighbouring properties, the van would have led the coppers straight to them. A generally weak specimen, Spazzer was already physically exhausted. His throat was raw; the burden of stolen goods banged painfully against his spine. But these minor problems were put into perspective when he emerged from the park's side gate onto Miry Lane, and saw that Tookey's van was now little more than a glistening white hump.

Spazzer slid to a halt, the two sacks slipping from his frozen fingers. For several seconds he could only stand there, gaping. Removing the canvas would clear the van's roof, windscreen and doors, but not the wheels, which were buried past their arches. A dull hollow feeling spread in his gut as it slowly dawned on him that this unforeseen problem had derailed the entire job. Even if they managed to find shovels from somewhere, how long would it take to dig the vehicle out, and how much attention would that attract? There were houses on Miry

Lane less than thirty yards away. Had he not already been shaking and soaked with sweat just from the five-minute run it had taken him to get here, he'd probably have been knocked sick by the realisation that all this work had now been for nothing. The only possibility was hiding the bags in the park, and coming back for them at a later date, but that was a big risk. In fact, it was a big enough risk leaving the van here, but there wasn't much choice there.

He glanced over his shoulder, half-expecting to see Tookey stumbling towards him. That there was no sign of his accomplice only aggravated Spazzer all the more. One thing was a definite: they could not hang around here any longer. He clumped wearily back the way he'd come, cursing under his breath. When he reached the north gate, his smoke-ravaged lungs were wheezing and he was furious that he still hadn't encountered Tookey headed the other way. He was also furious about the job going tits up – because that was the truth of it. The whole thing was fucked. The most they could take from here now was one bag each, because they were going to have to go the whole distance home on foot. It would be the poorest haul in God-knows how many jobs. He checked the road was still deserted before hurrying across, only to notice as he entered the drive that the house was no longer lit. He gazed up, baffled. Neither the angels on the roof nor the neon tubing along the eaves were aglow. The lights inside had also been switched off. Or, possibly, they'd fused. What the hell was Tookey playing at?

On approaching the front door, Spazzer found it closed and locked. But through the side-panel, one light was still visible inside, albeit faint and glimmering. He brushed the flakes from the diamond-paned glass to get a better look. Mid-way down the hall, a mass of fallen, smouldering foliage was heaped amid a tangle of black, twisted wires. He could vaguely make out what looked like a human form lying in it, though it was charred and crisp all over, and flames were still licking up and down it.

Spazzer's mouth was too dry even to emit a croak of horror. His spittle was like a rotten apple core as he tried to swallow it.

And if it wasn't his imagination that another faintly humanoid shape appeared to be laying alongside the first, wrapped around it in fact, this too blackened by burning, then he couldn't make any other sense of it. Spazzer turned away almost drunkenly; even through the closed door he could smell seared flesh. His heart then skipped a beat at the sight of the great, white inflatable bear rearing at him from the end of the side-passage – only for it to flop down onto all fours, and sag slowly inward on itself, its fearsome visage crinkling and shrivelling as heated air no longer rushed into it.

In a near-daze, Spazzer circled around the collapsing rubbery form and ran – though this time he *really* ran, with great, loping gazelle-like strides, down the drive, across the road and back through the park. At the end of Miry Lane he stopped to grab one of the bags he'd already brought, swung it to his shoulder and continued on his way, fear and horror giving him strength he'd never imagined he possessed, enabling him to cover the distance home in only fifteen minutes. Ironically, the snow had stopped falling by the time he reached the tenement where he lived. He made it up the four flights of switchback stairs without meeting anyone, entered his apartment, threw the bag into his bedroom and went through into the living room, sweating and shivering. There wasn't much in there: a badly sprung sofa, a TV and a low coffee table, the only accoutrements of which were a fresh packet of fags, a mug and a half-drunk bottle of whiskey. He necked four fingers swiftly and jammed a cig into his mouth. Almost absent-mindedly he switched the TV on, staring at a young and surprisingly desirable Julie Andrews dancing wildly with a bunch of cartoon animals. Barely seeing it, he poured another four fingers down his neck. Oblivion – that was the only solution. Turning the TV off, he took another swig of Scotch, this time straight from the bottle, and tottered towards his bedroom.

Spazzer wasn't sure what time it was, probably sometime in the early hours, when he finally woke. His head was muzzy from the whiskey, but his bedroom was ice-cold and his right eye was hurting him terribly.

He groped out blindly for the bedside light and yanked the cord. As the bulb came on, he felt at his face, finding blood on his cheek and what seemed to be a small sliver of wood insinuated into the corner of his eye. After he'd extricated it, he peered at it in disbelief. It was a tiny pink and white-striped candy cane.

Glancing down at his pillow, he saw the clockwork Santa laying there; one of its arms was missing and its neck twisted at a grisly angle, but its legs still pumped as if it were climbing the ladder. Spazzer was already past the stage of wonder and amazement. The sack of presents sat beside the bed, so that explained how the little bastard had got in here. He snarled as he snatched the figure up, hurled it to the floor and stomped on it again and again, cogs and springs scattering in all directions. When he'd finished, he scooped the flattened wreckage, stumbled through to the kitchen and thrust it down the waste disposal. But once the mechanism had finished clattering and chewing, reducing everything to mulch, he heard something else from his bedroom – it sounded like paper scrunching and tearing.

On hurrying back, he stopped in the open doorway, not knowing if he dared venture further. Various colourful packages had fallen from the sack and were moving about on the carpet of their own accord. Paper was slowly unravelling. It seemed that Spazzer had dealt with the Christmas decorations, but now he had the Christmas toys to face.

MIDNIGHT SERVICE

It wasn't snowing heavily but it was sufficient to cover the ground, and Capstick couldn't suppress an ironic grin. Every December, people hoped and prayed for a white Christmas, yet whenever one happened, the entire infrastructure of the United Kingdom seemed to fall apart. Offices closed early, trains got delayed and now, it seemed, bus journeys were cancelled.

"It's more than my job's worth to continue tonight," the chubby driver had announced after unexpectedly pulling off the main trunk road somewhere between Derby and Macclesfield, into a town whose name Capstick hadn't managed to catch. "We can't possibly risk these surfaces any more, and apparently the weather's going to get worse before it gets better."

Beyond the open entrance to the station garage, flakes fluttered down like dove feathers. Yet the crisp layer they'd formed on the roads and pavements was only carpet deep. *God help us if we lived in Canada or Siberia*, Capstick thought.

"Hey, whoa … I know it's a problem!" the driver added, turning defensively pink at the chorus of groans. "No-one wants this on Christmas Eve. I'm stuck here too. But it's my backside on the line if we have an accident. The company will do its best to fix you up with lodgings, but this bus can't go any further tonight.

Capstick, now trudging away from the coach station with satchel slung at his shoulder, had not bothered waiting to see what the company managed to come up with. No doubt some soulless motel on a motorway lay-by, with no bar, no restaurant and next to no staff. It would be just about bearable any other night of the year, and at the end of the day he probably didn't have a lot of alternative tonight either, but for the moment he was too angry to think straight, let alone stand around in that drab waiting-room and make polite conversation with people he didn't know.

But whichever town he'd been marooned in, it wasn't especially prepossessing. He'd expected it to resemble most other provincial towns at 10.30pm on Christmas Eve: hung with garish illuminations, crammed end-to-end with shouting, fighting, vomiting revellers. Well, the decorations were here, but the moronic mob wasn't. The streets were eerily empty as he prowled them; even the strands of multi-coloured lights zigzagging back and forth overhead and the snow crunching underfoot failed to create an atmosphere of cheer. There was an indelible dinginess about the buildings; they were old, sooty, and of varied shapes and styles, with no apparent thought given to the elegance and order that usually earmarked modern town-planning. Shops, factories and apartment houses stood side by side along every thoroughfare, all closed, all teetering over Capstick's head as he proceeded up steep, narrow alleys or down flights of winding, icy steps, his breath smoking, his fingers turning numb despite his woollen gloves.

Nowhere did he see a hotel sign or even a bed-and-breakfast, though God alone knew what any such accommodation would be like in this dump. Not that he'd had a great deal to look forward to anyway, if he was honest. It had been Gretchen's idea that he go and spend Christmas Day in Manchester, though he didn't know why she was so adamant about it. His family never had a pleasant thing to say about her, even though they hadn't once met her. Marlene would give him her usual frosty reception. His kids were now fourteen and sixteen, so it wasn't as if they *needed* their daddy present. But even if they did, Tabby was a teen terror whose aggressive selfishness infuriated him after just a few minutes (though Marlene seemed willing to endure any amount of it, which was probably half of the problem), while Tommy was a boorish oaf who had inherited right wing views from somewhere and yet never had any arguments to back them up.

On the subject of Gretchen, Capstick tried to call her for the third time, but again there was no answer. It wasn't particularly late – she would still be out with her friends, partying. He couldn't help feeling sour about that. He'd always known that getting involved with one of his students had the potential to create this kind of situation; her wanting to trip the light fantastic and him preferring to sit in front of the TV. She was no longer a student of course, but that age-gap was still there. An ugly thought occurred to him about why she was so ready to spend Christmas without him, but he shook it from his mind. The bigger problem at present was the cold. Never having expected to be outdoors, he was only wearing a lightweight jacket over his shirt. His trainers were already caked with ice crystals, which were fast melting through the rubber and canvas, soaking his socks and feet. It was pure good fortune that he had gloves, but they weren't much protection in truth. He'd wandered for quite some time by now, and probably wouldn't even be able to find his way back to the coach station. He glanced around, feeling more than a little concerned, but no fellow pedestrians were abroad to ask. The steadily falling snow muffled all sound, so even if there'd been someone on a nearby street, he wouldn't necessarily hear them. The occasional car swished by, but they were few and far between.

Capstick walked on, entering a small square, on the other side of which stood a row of spike-topped railings with an open gate in the middle, giving through to what looked like a yard enclosed by high buildings, though down at the far end of it a light was moving. It was only a glimmer; from this distance it looked like someone carrying a lantern. As Capstick watched, the clotted blackness down there split vertically as more light spilled through an opened door, widened further to admit the outline of a figure, then narrowed again and winked out. A faint *thump* was heard.

He approached the railings and peered across the yard. The building at the far end looked vaguely churchlike. It was too dark to see any real detail, but its roof was vaulted and there was a spire of some sort. Before he knew what he was doing, he was walking down towards it. Capstick hadn't been into a church for as long as he could remember, and had no religious beliefs. In fact, there was a time when he'd badmouthed Christianity at every opportunity, calling it "abusive superstition" and preferring to ignore the good things it did such as the provision of charity and shelter. Not that he was going to ask for either of those things now – good God, he wasn't that far gone! – but he could use some directions, and it wouldn't hurt to go indoors and get warm for a few minutes.

A high stained glass window on the right implied he was correct about the ecclesiastical purpose of this place, though there was no light behind it, making it look grimy, while several of its panes appeared to be missing. On the left, he passed what looked like a small memorial garden recessed between cliff-faces of brickwork. A central statue grinned at him from beneath a veil of icicles. One stone hand clutched an upright spear; the other extended forward, also covered in snow, but pointing downward.

When he reached the main entrance door, he saw a slogan painted in black on the whitewashed bricks above its lintel:

GOD IS JUST

Capstick turned the handle and shoved the door open.

He was confronted with a long, bare corridor lit by weak electric bulbs. The floor was flagged; the walls and ceiling made from painted plaster, which was much cracked and festooned in its high corners with clumps of dust-thick cobweb. At the far end, a female figure passed from sight through a half-open door.

Capstick stayed where he was, snowflakes gusting past him. The woman had been wrapped in a shawl and wearing a floor-length skirt and a coal-scuttle bonnet. Period costume? That seemed odd, though just now it didn't really matter. He closed the door, blocking out most of the bitter cold, though his breath still puffed in discernible clouds. To his left, there appeared to be a kind of porter's lodge, its open door exposing a row of empty coat-hooks. A little further along there was another door; warily, he advanced and glanced through it. This room boasted a white-tiled floor, clean metal surfaces and racks of gleaming utensils. He'd never heard of a church having a kitchen before, but maybe this was one of those all-in-one places, church and church hall together.

He wandered further along the corridor, passing another entrance on the right, beyond which a dark, narrow stair led upward, and approaching the door at the far end. When he pushed this, it swung open on a much larger room, which again made him think he was in a church hall. Its peeling plaster walls were covered with dog-eared notices and wads of age-yellowed paperwork. At one end, some kind of stage had been set up: a low wooden platform with a green baize curtain drawn across it. About ten rows of stiff-backed wooden chairs were arranged to face it, none currently occupied, though on a nearby shelf there was an old oil-lantern, possibly having just been deposited there by whoever Capstick had seen enter.

He ventured forward a few yards.

The room had been decorated for the season. Swags of evergreen were looped around the walls at just above head-height. A tall Christmas tree occupied one corner, hung with variously coloured baubles, bits of tinsel and streamers. More clusters of seasonal greenery were draped over the backs of each chair, while a lengthy sideboard down the left-hand side, no doubt a repository for teacups and plates of biscuits on normal occasions, had been laid with a crimson cloth and sported a dignified centrepiece: a large holly wreath sprouting four lighted candles. Pleasant enough, but Capstick couldn't help thinking it all a little tatty. This stuff had probably been stored in cardboard boxes for the last twelve months, no doubt in some dismal attic. He half-expected a spider or cockroach to emerge from the nearest bunch of mistletoe.

As he pondered this, the baize curtain twitched.

"Oh, hello?" he said, edging his way through the chairs towards the stage. "Look, I'm sorry for the intrusion, but I was wondering if you could help me?"

There was no response, but the curtain twitched again. Someone was definitely there.

"Hello?" Capstick repeated. Still there was no reply. Cautiously, he reached for the curtain.

"Can I help?" came a voice from behind.

Capstick spun around. A tall, lean figure in a gray suit and clerical collar, with a pale face and short sandy hair, had entered the hall behind him.

"Oh, I'm sorry ..." Capstick stammered, not sure whether to address the man as 'Father' or 'Reverend'. "But, well, this may sound a bit ridiculous ..."

"Gentleman of the road, are you?"

"What?" Capstick was startled. Surely he didn't look that bad? He brushed self-consciously at his beard. "Erm ... no, though I will admit to being lost."

"So many do at this festive time of year."

As the vicar wove his way forward through the seats, Capstick saw that he was actually quite old, his face wrinkled with a yellowish tinge, his eyes rheumy. His hair, which was colourless, was extraordinarily thin; it looked sandy from a distance because he'd greased the few lank strands of it that remained backward over his liver-spotted scalp. His suit, once smart, was dusty and crumpled.

"I'm stuck in town by accident," Capstick added, slightly distracted by this. "Trying to find some ... well, first of all, some accommodation. And secondly, some transport out of here."

"The first of those we can help you with ... of course we can." The vicar smiled, his bloodless lips drawn back on brownish pegs, and laced his fingers together. "The second, alas, no."

"I wasn't asking for a bed," Capstick replied hastily. "I'm perfectly willing to pay for a hotel, if you can put me in the right direction to find one."

"I'm not sure many of our local hotels will be open at this hour, Mr. …?"

"Capstick … Ronald Capstick."

The vicar nodded. He didn't offer his own name.

"None will be open at all?" Capstick said skeptically.

"By all means walk around the town and have a look, but we don't get many visitors here."

Can't imagine why, Capstick thought.

"As I say," the vicar said, "*we* can accommodate you."

Capstick glanced across the hall to a row of three tall, arched windows; snowflakes swirled in the black tumult beyond them. This probably wasn't the sort of offer he should turn down without at least some consideration.

"For a small indulgence," the vicar added.

"Sorry … indulgence?" It immediately struck Capstick how shortsighted he'd been to have mentioned that he had cash.

"I don't mean money," the vicar explained, eerily, as if he was a mind-reader. "The fact is you've arrived here just in the nick of time, Mr. Capstick. Christmas Eve is the occasion of our annual miracle play. This year, as every year, we're presenting the tale of the Derby Ram."

"Derby Ram?" Capstick was vaguely fazed by the odd turn in the conversation.

"It's a local story, so it doesn't surprise me that you haven't heard it. Doubtless there are different forms of mummery in your own town?"

"Doubtless." Capstick didn't know whether there were or weren't.

"The Derby Ram tells the tale of Old Tup, a magical ram, who brought great fortune to a poor farmer and his wife. But we are a little short-handed this year, so if *you* were to participate …?" The vicar regarded his guest with deep interest, though up close his eyes were so cloudy and jaundiced that it was amazing he could see anything.

"Excuse me?" Capstick said. "You're saying you want *me* to be in your play?"

"The ram is the easiest part. It has no lines."

"You want me to appear as Old …?"

"Old Tup, yes. It's a simple thing, I assure you. All you'll need do is wander up and down the stage in costume, behaving like, well …" those brown teeth again, "a beast of the field."

"And that's *all* I have to do?" Capstick meant the question to be ironic.

"It's a small thing, but it would mean a great deal to our audience."

Capstick glanced at the still-empty rows of seats. "Which will be who?"

"The orphans, of course."

Capstick looked at him askance. He hadn't realised that words like 'orphans' were still in use, but that wasn't his main source of puzzlement. "It's almost half past eleven. Isn't that rather late to be putting on a show for a bunch of children?"

"Christmas Eve is special, Mr. Capstick. The miracle play is the precursor to our traditional midnight service."

"Oh, yes, of course …"

The vicar's interlaced hands clenched until they were knots of sinew and bone. His stained eyeballs bulged in their sockets. “I beseech you to consider this. Christmas is all about giving, as they say.”

“Yes … sorry if I seem hesitant. I haven’t done this sort of thing very often.”

“Oh dear.”

“I don’t mean the giving bit. I mean …”

“I understand.” The vicar’s thin lips worked together. He looked too disappointed for words.

“But I don’t suppose it can hurt,” Capstick added, thinking he must be mad but asking himself what else he’d be doing with the remainder of his evening; it didn’t seem likely they’d have satellite television here and he’d almost finished his paperback during the bus journey.

The vicar’s face broke into another brown-toothed grin. “Excellent … truly excellent. You’ll find a bedroom you can use at the top of the stairs. I’ll have your costume sent up.”

“You’re sure I’ll only have to walk around on stage?”

“And dance a little.”

“Dance?”

“To amuse the orphans. A dancing animal. A comic thing.”

Capstick’s thoughts strayed to pantomime cows, pantomime horses – tediously unfunny icons of the annual festive farce. Horrendously embarrassing. But at least his face wouldn’t be seen. He glanced at his watch; it was twenty to twelve. “What time do we start?”

“In ten minutes.”

That was a relief. If the show had to wrap up before Midnight Mass, it couldn’t last for very long.

“I’d better get a move on,” Capstick said.

“Yes, freshen up, as the saying goes. Oh, and when you come back down, Mr. Capstick, use the back staircase. Wouldn't want you to come in through the actual audience."

"Of course. Any particular reason?"

"In your costume? Highly unprofessional."

Yes, because otherwise they'd think we were in the West End. Not that Capstick particularly wanted to jostle a path through a crowd of unruly urchins. "No problem. The back stairs."

But the front stairs presented problems enough. They were steep, creaky and unlit. He stumbled a couple of times as he ascended, on one occasion only his splayed hands preventing him landing face-first on the bare timber treads. It was only a little better on the next floor, where dim bulbs revealed another long passage, large patches of naked brick exposed where the plaster had rotted away. He regarded its numerous doorways helplessly; some were closed, some open. None gave any clue as to whether he'd find a bed behind them, though clearly there was someone else up here – because a whistling *smack*, the sound of a short, sharp impact, sounded from somewhere close by.

Several more such impacts sounded at regular intervals, and Capstick almost blundered over the edge of another staircase, even narrower, darker and steeper than the first – the 'back staircase' he supposed – before he finally traced their source to the door at the landing's farthest, dimmest end. When he pushed this one open, frigid streetlight filtering through a tall window revealed what looked like a long-disused schoolroom: a blackboard still with faint chalk etchings upon it; several all-in-one desks and chairs; a tall stool in a corner, where dunces once sat. Nothing stirred save a few threads of twisting dust. Thinking he'd made a mistake, Capstick crossed the passage to the door on the other side, but this opened on a more cavernous and yet equally desolate space. The window at its far end was arched and contained fragments of stained glass. Its floorboards were sprung and its central aisle, which led away between pews, crisscrossed by fallen beams. If there was a faint, rasping snicker from some unseen corner in there, Capstick chose to ignore it.

He backtracked along the corridor, now seeing that another room stood open and that light shone out from it. He wasn't sure how he'd missed it before, but when he glanced inside, he saw six iron-framed beds, three ranged to each side. One had been made up with a mattress, pillow and blankets. On inspection, these proved to be fresh, while the room, though basic – bare floorboards, bare plaster – was at least clean.

Capstick closed the door, dumped his satchel and crossed to the window. Decades of dead flies lay along its sill, but beyond it billions of flakes danced over the chimneys and black, slanted roofs. Directly below lay another snow-filled yard. A narrow passage led off from it, a barred gate standing at its far end. He half expected to see a coach-and-four trundle by on the other side, but in fact an ordinary Bedford van drove past, reminding him that normal life wasn't too far away – if he could just get through tonight's nonsense.

There was a sound outside his bedroom door: a low whispering. He turned, expecting a knock. Was this his curtain call?, he wondered without enthusiasm. But no knock followed. Instead there was another of those rasping snickers. Irritated, he strode across the room, but before he reached the door he heard the dull thunder of smallish feet scampering away. When he yanked the door open, there was no-one on the landing. Presumably this meant the orphans had arrived. As he closed the door again, he supposed he ought to be feeling more charitable: for homeless kids, abandoned kids – 'undomiciled' was probably one of the in-phrases these days – Christmas Eve was bound to be an exciting time. A special show and then Midnight Mass. Yeah, great. Perhaps they'd get a tangerine each as a real treat.

There was a loud knock.

"Okay, the joke's over," he said aggressively, leaping back to the door and lugging it open.

Again the landing was deserted, but now the door opposite stood ajar, and what looked like a mass of dirty lamb's wool hung from its handle. When Capstick examined it more closely, he realised that this was his costume. The fleece was real, and by the size of it had come from a fairly hefty animal, but it was also rather repulsive: it smelled of sweat and was odiously stained, while the headpiece was crude and synthetic, a stitched cotton hood onto which additional fragments of fleece had been fixed with heavy staples. The same applied to the twisting plastic horns attached one to either temple. When Capstick tried it on, it was very uncomfortable, the hood tight, the staples pressing hard against his scalp, and the eye-slits too small for him to see out of them clearly. With a grunt, he wrestled it off, and in his efforts, brushed against the half-open door, which now opened all the way.

Beyond it was a long room, again weakly lit, but with a rack of old clothing running down its centre. At first Capstick wondered if these were other costumes, before realising that they were more likely give-aways: suits, dresses, jackets and coats, all shabby and rather grubby, though no doubt they'd be dry-cleaned and pressed before being donated. There were also several shelves: the highest was laden with hats, the two lower ones crammed with shoes and boots. And then he saw something else: an old signpost leaning against the wall near the window. It was clearly ancient, its timber uprights rotted clean through, its main placard so blistered by damp and eaten by moss that its flaking letters were almost indecipherable:

CK RTH GREEN
UN ON
WORKHOU E

Amazed, he backed out onto the landing – where he found that several of the lights had failed, including those over the main staircase and in the room where he'd be sleeping. At least, he assumed they'd failed. He doubted there was a timer in a forgotten pile like this. Either way, they'd plunged all but his immediate surroundings into blackness. Not that it mattered. He'd already decided there was no way he could spend the night here. Once this fiasco downstairs was done, he'd say his goodbyes and go looking for the nearest police station. If they couldn't put him in the direction of a motel, no-one could. He groped his way to the top of the back staircase, the ram's costume bundled under his arm, and, determined not to listen out for any other odd sounds from the derelict chapel, descended as hurriedly as he dared.

But it was ludicrously dark. There didn't seem to be any windows down there, not even small ones. On one hand this shouldn't surprise him: he knew all about the old workhouses and how they'd been designed to be as uncomfortable as possible to deter all but the most desperate poor; but on the other hand, if someone insisted on re-adapting one of those aged buildings for more modern use, was it asking too much that they update it a little? At the bottom of the stairs, he blundered into a damp, musty hanging, and only when he struggled past that did he at last see light: Christmas firelight shimmering around what looked like tall sections of flat, theatrical scenery. He shrugged his ram's costume onto his shoulders as he sidled his way through. Somewhere ahead, he could hear whispers and titters of anticipation. It seemed the audience was in place.

Then a woman stepped into his path.

He recognised her as the woman he'd seen earlier. Her costume was rustic Victorian – that ground-length skirt, that shawl, that coal-scuttle bonnet from beneath which wisps of stringy, metal-gray hair protruded. But like Reverend What's-His-Name, she was incredibly old, her face wizened as desiccated leather, her mouth a toothless, crumpled maw, her eyes milky, sightless orbs.

Capstick didn't know what else to say. "Erm … hello."

She simply stared at him – if she could even see him, which he doubted. He realised that someone else was talking.

"… the ever-popular Christmas Eve custom …" came a muffled voice.

"Excuse me." Capstick shouldered past his comatose fellow-thespian, and found himself a position from where he could see onto the stage. The green baize drapes had now been pulled aside and a row of candles – a fire hazard if ever he'd seen one – flickered along the front of the stage. Rev. What's-His-Name was already out there. He too had donned rustic period attire: a doublet, breeches and heavy boots, with a leather apron worn over the top. He stood with one foot on a block of wood, as he continued his address.

"… of the Derby Ram."

There was no immediate response, and Capstick wondered if this was supposed to be his cue.

"Of the Derby Ram!" What's-His-Name said again, with a hint of impatience.

Hastily, Capstick pulled the odorous hood down over his face, but before he could fix it properly, a firm shove between his shoulder-blades – presumably from the old woman – sent him tottering out onto the stage. Immediately, there were titters and snickers from the auditorium, though Capstick could see almost nothing beyond the immediate pall of dusty candlelight, partly because the mask was so ill-fitting but also because all the other lights in the hall had been turned off. The audience was present, however; when he looked closely, the candle-flames glinted green and scarlet from a plethora of Christmas baubles and ornaments. He imagined the young hoodlums pillaging the decorations as they came in, using them for necklaces, earrings, hats.

"Ahhh … and here he is." What's-His-Name held out a hand of welcome.

Capstick moved awkwardly forward. As he did, a dull, squeaky music track commenced: something very folksy, played on an accordion, but clearly an ancient recording as it was fogged by scratches, crackles and a repeating agonised hiss rather like a life-support machine in a hospital.

What's-His-Name started to sing in a creaky, warbling tone, telling the tale of a journey to Derby, during which a ram was encountered, "the finest fed on hay".

Remembering what he was supposed to be doing, Capstick began a clumsy dance, to which there were renewed titters and chuckles. Thank God no-one here knew him. Otherwise, he'd never live this down. Even so, he capered back and forth across the stage, attempting to stay in time with the music.

What's-His-Name continued his nonsense ditty, describing the bovine wonder as standing at least ten yards tall. Capstick still caught only fleeting glimpses of his surroundings, so he didn't notice that a third person had come onto the stage until he almost barged into her: it was the old woman. She was dancing too, but more elegantly than he was, arms outspread, skirts swirling as she turned delicate pirouettes. She was remarkably lithe given her age, though an explanation for this struck him as he blundered away from her. In fact it was rather obvious. She was in costume too – as the farmer's wife. That hideous, hag-like visage was almost certainly a mask.

Meanwhile, What's-His-Name continued to spin his ludicrous tale, extolling the virtues of a brute whose skull was so broad that a pulpit might be built there from which a parson could preach, and now taking Capstick by the hand and leading him towards the front of the stage. Capstick went meekly, still unsure what he was supposed to do, though cautious of getting too close to the naked flames; he imagined this musty old costume would go up like a Roman candle. As the reverend gentleman went on to describe how the ram, when stood with legs athwart, could cover four whole acres of land, he pressed down on Capstick's shoulder. Feeling even more foolish, but eager to comply and get this awful experience over, Capstick went down on all fours. It was because he couldn't see clearly that he head-butted the wooden block on the floor.

"Damn!" he grunted, and at the same time, from the corner of his eye, spotted the old woman twirling gracefully along the front of the stage towards him with something shiny in her hand.

What's-His-Name was now singing about a butcher's boy being drowned in blood.

But Capstick wasn't listening. He didn't at first believe that the thing the old woman was carrying was a real knife – and then he saw its edge gleaming, and he reacted in kneejerk fashion, springing up from his supine position and retreating from the pair of them. The music immediately ceased. Hisses and snarls sounded from beyond the curtain of candlelight. There was a rustle of sharp movements; festive baubles glittered.

Capstick wrenched off the headpiece and hurled the costume on the stage. "What the hell is this?"

"Why, the tradition of the Derby Ram, Mr. Capstick." What's-His-Name's sickle grin split his face from ear to ear, the palsied flesh wrinkling back as if this too was no more than a clever mask; his brown peg teeth looked inches long. "And its ritual slaughter."

The old woman came on swiftly, the knife, curved and gleaming, raised above her head. Capstick spun and fled towards the wings, to an immediate accompaniment of banging, scraping chairs in the auditorium. Beyond the theatrical flats, he spied a low flight of steps with a door at the bottom. The rumble of dozens of feet on the stage spurred him down towards it. Beyond that lay a warren of dingy brick passages, again only half-lit, caked with dust, strewn with rags and bones. He blundered madly, turning left and right, feeling an icy breeze on his face but uncertain which direction it came from. Another door appeared. He dashed through it into a lengthy wainscoted room where several benches and trestle tables had been laid out as though for dinner, though there was no tablecloth, no napkins – just gnarled wooden surfaces, two-pronged forks and sharp, serrated knives. Fleetingly, Capstick recalled a question he'd unconsciously put to himself upstairs: if the chapel here was derelict, where was the midnight service to be held?

Now he knew – because it clearly wasn't going to be a church service.

With hisses and cackles echoing in the corridors behind, he fled across the room, knocking tables and benches askew. At the far side was yet another door. This one opened on a large entrance hall, its flagged floor wet from the recent passage of multiple feet, snowflakes blowing along it. Glancing right, Capstick saw why: beneath a heavy stone arch, it opened to the outside. Thanking God, he ran in that direction, screaming for help … only to realise once out there that he'd made a drastic mistake.

Enough star-lit snow crusted the upturned earth, leaning headstones and fallen, ice-crabbed angels to reveal three high walls hemming him in.

He turned and backed away, half-stumbling, only vaguely aware that he mustn't fall into any of the muddy cavities yawning on every side. As they milled out from beneath the arch to encircle him, he realised that he'd made another mistake. The green and scarlet glints from the auditorium had not denoted candle-flames reflecting from their Christmas baubles – but from their eyes.

THE FAERIE

When they reached higher ground, the sleet transformed to snow and Arthur began to worry. Of course, he didn't say anything.

Gabby was seated in the front passenger seat, chattering away. When the green swathes of moor to either side suddenly turned white and the windscreen started filling up with solid flakes rather than globs of watery ice, she squeaked with excitement.

"Daddy, it's snowing. It's snowing properly. Look!"

Arthur nodded, and made a mental note not to mention that they still had over twenty miles to go, which included High Peak, and that, to make matters worse, it was now close to four o'clock and getting dark as well. Suddenly, taking the back roads to throw Moira off the scent didn't seem so smart a move.

"That means Santa will definitely come this year, doesn't it?" Gabby said.

"Santa comes every year, even if it's not snowing."

"Well he hasn't been every year. I mean, not *every* year."

"No," Arthur agreed. "But he will this year. I promise."

The child seemed content with that and sat humming for a few moments, before saying: "Mummy doesn't believe in Santa."

"I know."

"She always says he's a furry story – like in that book you bought for my birthday last year."

Arthur said nothing, but smiled a little. At Moira's insistence, Gabby was a painfully well-spoken child, yet now and then – when pronouncing the word 'fairy' for example – her Manchester accent came through. His smile was tinged with sadness of course. He didn't want to remember the trouble that present had caused; a simple book of fairy tales.

"But I believe in him anyway," Gabby added. "Does Auntie Lucy believe in him?"

"Oh yes, absolutely."

"He will know I'm spending Christmas at Auntie Lucy's, won't he? What if he takes my presents to Manchester and I'm not there?"

"You'll get your presents, don't worry."

But Arthur was increasingly distracted from the conversation. Snow was driving hard into the windscreen; visibility was being drastically reduced. He fiddled with the radio to see if he could find some weather updates. But the storm seemed to be interfering with that as well; all he heard was the crackle of static, the *thudding* of his wipers.

He peered ahead, straining his eyes. The bleak moorland they'd been traversing for so long had been completely obliterated. Even the single-lane tarmac road was disappearing; its central portion, like a long, dark ribbon, was still visible, but the snow was encroaching on it from either side, steadily covering it over – which annoyed him as well as worried him. Okay, Britain's weather was sporadic and unpredictable. But this was December for Christ's sake! And they were in the Peak District! Was it asking too much of the local authorities that they send their gritting trucks out every day at this time of year, just to be on the safe side? He was forced to slow the car down. Soon they were crawling along at twenty.

"Why are you staying with Auntie Lucy anyway?" Gabby asked. "Is it because you're working there again?"

"That's right," he replied.

Several other times when he'd left Moira, Arthur had excused his temporary residence at his sister's in Sheffield by telling his daughter that he had a contract there. Of course, at seven years old, Gabby was too young to know what the junior partner in an accountancy firm did, or that, as his office was back in Manchester, he didn't earn anything when he made these lonely sojourns over the mountains. In that respect, how on Earth he was going to provide the presents Gabby was expecting this Christmas he didn't know. Not, if he was honest, that he really believed she'd be with him over Christmas. On the previous occasions when he'd fled home, he'd done it alone. Moira hadn't bothered to come and find him. She'd known where he was and had rung him up to jeer down the telephone, but now that he had their daughter in tow things would be different. He glanced at his mobile phone on the dashboard. He'd switched it off but didn't doubt there'd be twenty messages logged on it already, each one more angry and threatening than the last. He shuddered at the thought and tried to concentrate on the road again. But it was difficult. By turning the phone off, he'd only been delaying the inevitable. With Gabby gone, there was no chance Moira would confine her response to verbal wrath. Almost certainly she'd come over to Sheffield personally, probably in the next day or so. No matter how severe this winter storm became, the A57 would stay open, and, even if it didn't, Moira would find some way over to Yorkshire.

He fiddled with the radio again. Still there was nothing, just white noise.

The irony of that phrase made him laugh nervously.

"Are *you* looking forward to Christmas, Daddy?" Gabby asked, interested to hear what sounded like a moment of merriment from him.

"I am, but remember it's two weeks off yet. We've a lot to do before then."

Arthur felt a pang of guilt. Even though he knew it was in the child's best interests for him to pretend that everything was okay, it was difficult leading her on so much. The trouble with deceit was that it led to more deceit, and more, until there was nothing else.

"I just can't help it," she said. "I get so excited."

He tried to smile. "It's okay to get excited."

"Mummy doesn't think so. Do you remember last Christmas Eve, when she sent me to bed early because she said I was going to make myself sick?"

"Yes, I do."

He felt sick himself at the memory. That had been so like Moira. And so like *him* for not intervening.

He looked back through the years, and tried to work out when it was that his wife had morphed into such a stern, humourless bully – not just where Gabby was concerned, but where *he* was concerned too. She'd never thought him much of a masculine man, he knew that. Her father had been a retail giant, a big, gruff, cigar-chomping man's man, a pin-striped tyrant of the boardroom. That was the role model she'd grown up with. But it was only in recent years, and they'd been married for twelve, that she'd started to find her husband's lack of ambition tiresome. Okay, he was forty-three and still only a junior partner. He turned over a reasonable salary, but not as much as he was capable of. He was a quiet chap by nature, shy, retiring. He'd never worn the pants in their domestic life, but it was only since Moira had inherited the ownership of two sizeable department-stores from her late father, both of which she'd made even more successful, that she'd become openly antagonistic towards him. Not that they argued much. Arthur tended to take it all on the chin, apart from the odd occasion when it simply became unbearable and he packed his bags and went to stay for a few weeks at Lucy's. Mind you, it did seem a little pathetic, running off to his big sister's just because his wife had shouted at him.

"Oooh, where do we go to now?" Gabby suddenly asked.

Arthur had to slam the brakes on, sending the car into a ten-metre skid (thank God they'd only been crawling). When they stopped, he stared blankly at the road ahead. It appeared to fork. Faintly visible through the swirls of snowflakes, two minor tracks led off in opposite directions. There was no signpost on view.

Puzzled, he dug into the glove compartment to check the map. But unfortunately it was now too dark inside the car to read the wretched thing. When he put the interior light on, it affected little more than a dull glow, and his eyes weren't up to the rigours of scanning a crumpled, coffee-stained page on which the roads were squiggles and the names of the few settlements in this region printed so small that they'd be difficult to pick out with a magnifying glass. He glanced through the window again.

Whiteout conditions persisted, and night was now falling properly.

They'd gone wrong somewhere, which meant he now had a big decision to make. Either he chanced one of the two narrow tracks, both of which looked like farm roads, or he made a three-point turn – if such a thing was possible without getting stuck – and headed back. It probably wouldn't be snowing this hard on lower ground, but of course going back meant a confrontation with Moira. The prospect of that was almost worse than the thought of being marooned in a blizzard.

Arthur cursed himself for his timidity. He gazed at Gabby, demure and petite in her mittens and knitted coat, and, with her pretty looks and chestnut hair squared-off pageboy style, so like her mother. Though, while Gabby was affable and easy-going, Moira was awkward and brusque; while Gabby was patient and understanding, Moira was ill-tempered; while Gabby always saw the funny side of things, Moira – if the mood was on her – could be stingingly unamused. But all this was a distraction. What mattered now was the decision he came to in the next few minutes. As things were, it was nice and warm inside the car. But there was only about a quarter of a tank of fuel left, and if they got caught in a drift somewhere, the heating system would use that up fairly quickly. It certainly wouldn't last them through the night.

"Why don't we just go left?" Gabby said brightly.

"Why left?"

"Whenever you see signs on the road, they always say 'Keep Left'."

Arthur wanted to chuckle at his daughter's simple innocence, but another pang of guilt and worry went through him. Her comment only served to underline how precious she was, and how foolish he'd been to bring her up here on a whim. Now that he considered it, he wasn't even sure *why* he'd brought her.

He started driving again, bearing left. There was no particular reason why he went that way, but one route seemed as good as another. Both roads were now under several inches of pristine snow, and his tyres crunched noisily as he progressed. All he could see through the windscreen was a depthless pattern of flakes, though beyond the glow of his headlights this quickly receded into blackness.

If he was truthful with himself, the reason he'd brought Gabby was a negative one. It certainly hadn't been for her sake. Though she was excited by the idea of spending Christmas at her Aunt Lucy's, more likely she'd be spending it at home in the care of a sole parent who'd be even more sullen and irritable than usual. No, the reality was that he'd brought the child with him to try and punish Moira. It was too easy for him to just keep absconding alone. It had never seemed to bother his wife anyway. She just laughed at him, knowing full well that he'd eventually come back like a whipped dog. Well this time, he'd decided, it would be different. He'd wanted her to feel what he so often felt: bereft, desolated. He'd wanted to frighten her as well as upset her; he'd wanted her to realise that she'd finally pushed him too far, that he was capable of retaliation.

So that was what this was, he realised with a chill: revenge. Maybe you could even call it a kidnapping.

Of course, he'd never intended to bring his daughter into danger; the predicament they were in now was the result of bad luck. But it had served no real purpose to take Gabby to Lucy's; it had been an action designed purely to hurt, which, as Arthur listened to the shrill whistle of the wind, seemed like a colossal and portentous error.

"Daddy, a house!" the child suddenly squealed. "Look! All lit up!"

Arthur was now having trouble just keeping the car in a straight line. It was constantly sliding, its wheels threatening to lock. He imagined the axles and wheel-arches caked with ice. So it was a huge relief now to crane his neck up and see that Gabby wasn't mistaken. To their left, on high ground, a building was visible. At first, half obscured, it looked like a barn: tall, narrow, with a bleak, functional exterior made from weathered limestone. But, from its well-lit windows, it was more likely a barn-conversion.

He steered to the side of the road. They eased to a halt and sat there, gazing up. The house was now directly above them. Thanks to the flurrying flakes, much of it was still hidden, but Arthur's guess looked to have been correct. It was about the size of an old barn, but its windows – in particular the two bay windows at the front – though mullioned, were almost certainly a recent installation. The mellow light that flooded out of them was extremely comforting.

"Come on," he said, unfastening his seatbelt and zipping his anorak up.

He switched the engine off, and they climbed out of the car together. Initially the wind took their breath away; it had a sword's edge, and a sword straight from the Pole. Snowflakes fluttered in their faces like moths as they fought their way up a tall flight of steps, which, thanks to each tread being several inches deep, were highly treacherous.

At the top, they advanced along a short path – only visible as a linear and slightly sunken section of snow –

until they saw the front door. It was impressively tall and wide, with a carved pediment over the lintel; it looked like a symbol of the sun with a tree growing against it. The door itself was of solid oak with a big brass knocker.

"It's a grand-looking place," Arthur said. "Can't think what it's doing all the way out here in the wilds of Derbyshire."

He reached for the knocker, but the door creaked open as soon as he touched it.

They glanced through, and saw an arched stone passage with low wooden beams across its ceiling. It ended at a flight of four broad steps, which led up into a living area. A rosy flush of firelight was visible up there, and a pleasant scent struck their nostrils, a combination of oranges and cinnamon, and something else: evergreens. The reason for that soon became obvious. The beams in the entrance hall had been decked for Christmas: alternating strands of ivy and holly had been woven around them. The only sound was a distant crackle of flames.

To Arthur it was extremely welcoming, but Gabby had different ideas.

Oddly, she began to tug on his arm, trying to draw him away. "We should go, Daddy. We should go right now."

He glanced down at her, puzzled. "What're you talking about?"

"I bet it's the furry house," she said.

"What?"

"It was in that book you got me. It said that out on the moors, when people are lost, the furry house comes and the people go inside and think they're safe. And the furry house disappears, and they go with it. And they're never seen again."

Arthur chuckled and tapped on the door-jamb with his knuckles. "Darling, this isn't a fairy house. Look, it's as solid as you and me."

"That doesn't mean anything. They have to look real to trap people."

"Don't be daft."

"I'm not being daft."

"Look, I know I encourage you to believe in Santa, but you have to be realistic as well. This is not a fairy house, and even if it was, all I'm doing is asking directions. We're obviously lost and we can't just keep following that road, or we'll end up getting stuck. Okay?"

They gazed at each other solemnly, then finally, reluctantly, Gabby nodded.

"Okay. Come on then."

"Wait," she suddenly said. "Why's the door open? Aren't they frightened of robbers?"

"I don't expect they get many robbers all the way up here," Arthur replied. He shuddered as another gust of wind blasted past them, casting feather-sized flakes over their shoulders. "Look – come on in, we'll catch our death."

Gabby looked worried again, even alarmed. "We can't just go inside."

"I've told you, all I'm doing is asking where we are." This time he was more forceful, and led her in by the hand whether she liked it or not. "Hello?" he said loudly, as they advanced up the hall. "Anyone home?"

They climbed the stairs into the living area, which was luxuriously warm and very spacious. There were further ceiling beams, while the floor was of smoothly varnished wood with a woven rug in the middle portraying a forest scene in green and gold. At the far end was an immense chimney breast with a huge fireplace in it. This was stacked with logs, which hissed and spat as flames licked through them. To either side of it were deep leather armchairs, red in colour, while a leather sofa was further back and positioned to face a wall on which there hung a widescreen plasma TV, currently switched off. The curtains were drawn back on both bay windows, revealing the blizzard outside, though in front of one of these stood a tall spruce fir frosted with fake snow and hung with tasteful white ornaments: stars, icicles and other winter emblems.

There were more evergreens; not just garlanding the roof beams but arranged along the mantel and tucked in behind the curtain rails and television. On an elaborately carved sideboard, a lit candle stood among a generous pile of figs, apples and chestnuts.

Despite the homeliness of the scene, Gabby backed away again. "Daddy, let's go."

Arthur thought he understood why. It was vaguely Germanic in appearance, and probably reminded her of every depiction she'd ever seen of the woodland cottage in Hansel and Gretel, though without the confectionary.

"This is definitely the furry house," she said querulously.

He laughed. "Try to pronounce the word properly, eh. It's 'fairy', not 'furry'."

"I said 'furry'."

He crouched down, as much to reassure her as to educate her. "No, listen – think of how it's spelled: F.A.E.R.I.E."

"It doesn't look like that in the book."

"I know, but that's the way it should be spelled and pronounced. It's actually a very old and mysterious word …"

"Can I help you?" someone asked curtly.

Arthur stood up sharply, Gabby ducking behind him.

It was a woman, who had clearly just got out of a bath or shower. She was barefoot, wearing a silken green house-robe tied at the front with a strap, and in the process of towelling dry her long, glossy black hair. She was handsome and shapely, probably in her early thirties, and by the look on her face, which was a combination of bewilderment and annoyance, was a far cry from the faerie figure that Gabby had expected. In fact, at the sight of this perfectly normal person, Arthur felt his daughter relax and emerge into the open again.

"I'm terribly sorry," he said. "I don't mean to intrude, but the door was open."

"And?" The woman still looked far from happy.

"Er, well, sorry … the name's Crook, Arthur Crook." He offered a hand, which she ignored. "This is my daughter, Gabby. We're, er …"

"We're lost," Gabby piped up.

"Oh." The woman's expression softened slightly.

Arthur tried to laugh. "I suppose that happens quite a lot up here, eh?"

"Well," the woman said, "people don't often get as lost as *this*. We pride ourselves on being quite inaccessible."

"It's been a long drive, I must admit. And then the weather closed in."

"Where are you trying to get to?"

"Sheffield," Gabby said. "We're going to my auntie's."

"Are you?" The woman now smiled. "Well I think you're going to be late. Sheffield's that way," and she pointed in a direction that seemed the exact opposite of the one they'd been taking. "It's twenty-five miles at least."

"Ah," Arthur said, thinking again about the ferocity of the blizzard.

"Something tells me you aren't going to make it there tonight," the woman added.

"No," he admitted. "I could do with letting my sister know, I suppose." But he was reluctant to go back outside and turn his mobile on; the mere thought of the enraged messages that would assault his ears was harrowing. "I don't suppose I could use …"

"Our phone? I'm sorry, we don't have one."

"Oh. Well, I'm sorry to have troubled you. I suppose we'll just have to go back."

"Going back may not be the answer to your problems either." The woman moved past them, went lithely down the stairs and closed the front door. "Not if, when you say 'going back', you mean going back to the A57. I assume that's where you've come from?"

"Yes, it is."

"Well, the road between here and there is often blocked in conditions like these."

Arthur felt distinctly awkward. He didn't know what else to say.

"It's possible a snowplough will be sent up at some point," the woman added, returning to the lounge. "From Edale. But there's no guarantee. It happens from time to time when the weather changes unexpectedly. I don't suppose it looks good for the County Council if too many people get stuck up here and die."

"No, I don't suppose it does."

"Look, why don't you relax. Take your coats off and sit down beside the fire. I'm hardly going to throw you out, am I?"

"It's terribly nice of you … I mean we've just turned up on your doorstep."

"Don't worry about it." She took their coats. "Make yourselves at home. I won't be a minute."

They did as she said, still a little dazed by the speed of events. When the woman returned, Arthur had expected her to have got changed, but all she'd put on was a pair of gold slippers with curved Persian toes. Aside from that, she was still in her flimsy green robe, which clung to her full figure in all the right places. She was more than handsome, Arthur realised. In fact, with her delicate cheekbones, bright blue eyes and lustrous black hair, she was startlingly beautiful. She was also proving to be the perfect hostess.

She laid a tray down on a small table. From this, she handed Gabby a big mug of hot chocolate. "Something to warm you up," she said, smiling. Also on the tray was an ornate silver teapot, from which she poured a dark steaming liquid into a tall goblet. This she handed to Arthur. "My own Yuletide concoction," she explained. "Ragwort tea. Oh, don't worry. It's not actually made from ragwort – we call it that for a joke. It's red wine with apple, jasmine and cinnamon. And it's best served smoking hot."

Arthur sampled it, and had to admit that, though it was indeed 'smoking hot' – at first it made him wince – it was delectable.

"Can I get you something to eat?" the woman asked.

"Oh we couldn't, really."

"It's no trouble. We don't get the opportunity to entertain very often." And she was off again, presumably back to her kitchen.

"These are lovely decorations," Gabby commented, a thin moustache of chocolate occupying her top lip. "When are we going to put ours up, Daddy?"

"I don't know. I don't know what we're going to do." And if he was honest, he wasn't too worried at that moment. The room was lovely and warm, he was comfortably seated and the ragwort tea – even if it was only a fortified mulled wine – was slipping down like nectar.

"Oh!" the child exclaimed. "There are no furry lights … I mean *faerie* lights."

"That's better."

"There's no tinsel either. Why not?"

"Beats me." His eyes roved across rich loops of evergreen studded with berries and pinecones. They glistened in every corner of the room; their sappy fragrance was intoxicating. "There's a kind of green, eco feel to all this. Perhaps that explains why these people live all the way out here."

"You mean they're conservationists?"

He glanced down at her. "How do you know that word?"

"We've done it at school. Mrs. Higgins in Year Three says we are the future of the planet, and that it'll be our job to put it back in harmony with nature."

"Your teacher sounds like she knows what she's talking about," came the woman's voice, as she strolled back into view carrying a tray of food.

"Good grief," Arthur stuttered when it was placed down in front of them.

"I hope this is okay," the woman said. "We've got leeks in hot butter, grilled sausages with cherry and mustard relish, and cheddar and cranberry wedges with sweet biscuits. Oh, and that's a blue cheese with onion chutney, in case you haven't got a sweet tooth."

"You've prepared this just now?" Arthur said. "For *us*?"

"It's only a snack."

"A snack?"

"It's nothing. Enjoy it, please." She moved away back to her kitchen, taking Gabby's empty mug.

Arthur gazed after her. "She reminds me of Nigella Lawson."

"Nigella who?" Gabby asked.

"You know, the Domestic Goddess?"

"No."

"Forget it."

They ate hungrily, finding the food delicious. And when they'd finished, the woman reappeared to clear up. Before she did, she poured Arthur another goblet of ragwort tea, refusing to hear from him that he'd had enough.

Though he wasn't sure if such a creature had ever existed, Arthur had long yearned to roll back the years to that lost era when the perfect wife, as well as being an expert cook and housekeeper, was also gorgeous and alluring. Their hostess fulfilled these criteria spectacularly, particularly the last. She still wore that clingy green house-robe and was almost certainly naked underneath. It afforded constant glimpses of cleavage and thigh. Her hair hung past her shoulders in gleaming, raven tresses; her eyes and lips sparkled. It was enough to make him regret that he'd ever met Moira, let alone married her. His wife was an attractive woman in her own right; she always made an effort to look good. But it was all power-dressing with Moira, all dominance and submission. She was a severe beauty, and a cold one as well; they hadn't been intimate for several years. Now that Moira had her daughter, it was almost as if she'd done with such frivolities. And as for the cooking part, she'd long ago given up on that. These days they tended to go to restaurants, where almost certainly meals would be sent back and waiters chastised for taking too long.

"Do you think she's married?" Gabby asked, after the woman had removed the last of their crockery.

"How would I know?" Arthur took another sip of ragwort tea: it was heady and sweet, but made him feel very relaxed.

"She said 'we' and 'our' a couple of times."

"Yes, she did." It was difficult not to be depressed by that realisation.

"Maybe her husband's at work," Gabby said. "Normally you and mummy would still be at work at this time."

Arthur made no reply. It was an ugly reminder of that day's lunchtime, when he'd called unexpectedly at the child-minder's and collected Gabby without prearrangement. The child-minder, a thin, middle-aged woman with pinched features, had been very suspicious, almost as if Moira had trained her in advance not to trust her charge's father. Not that it mattered much now; he glanced at the window, where the snow, like something from a Dickensian pastiche, was gathering in the corner of each mullioned pane.

"If he's still at work now," Arthur said, "he won't be coming home tonight."

And that was a pleasant thought – which rather shocked him. He glanced at the dark liquor swirling in his goblet; he must be getting drunk.

A few moments passed, Arthur continuing to sip and Gabby wandering around the room, peeking at its sumptuous fixtures and fittings, finally settling down on her knees in front of the hearth. Like most children unused to real home fires, she was fascinated by the dancing flames.

"I suppose we should introduce ourselves," came their hostess's voice. Both father and daughter glanced around. They hadn't realised she had returned and was now seated in an armchair. "I'm Phoebe."

"That's … that's a nice name," Arthur replied, slurring slightly.

She laughed. "I hate it. I can think of three or four others I'd rather use. You said you were Arthur, didn't you?"

"Er … yes."

"I didn't realise anyone was called Arthur these days."

"My family were a bit old-fashioned, I suppose."

"Well there's nothing wrong with it. Arthur's a strong name, a hero's name."

"That isn't me, I'm afraid."

"Oh?"

"I'm no warrior. I'm no good at confrontation at all."

"You were brave enough to come up here."

"No, I was foolish. If we hadn't met you, Heaven knows where Gabby and I would be now."

She switched her gaze to the child. "Gabby's very sweet."

Gabby, who was still kneeling beside the fire, was clearly listening, but didn't reply.

"We only came this way because we're running from something," Arthur admitted. "Or rather … *I'm* running from it."

"I didn't mean to pry," Phoebe said. "You don't have to tell me any of this."

"No, it's all right. Why not?" And he took another sip of tea, a big one this time. "You say Gabby's sweet? She is, but her mother was sweet once."

"Ahh, I see."

"I don't think you do." He shook his head, which was feeling distinctly muzzy. "I suspect you're one of these people, Phoebe, who believes that only women can get trapped in abusive relationships. Am I right?"

"No. I think both sexes can equally be victimised. In fact, I *know* they can."

"Let me tell you, Phoebe," and he made a big gesture, sloshing drink down the front of his shirt. "My wife – dear God, I sound like a 1970s comedian, don't I! – my wife has a motor inside her. She's totally driven. Do you see what I mean?"

"Yes."

"Everything must be just so. And woe betide you if it isn't. Well, woe betide me. I mean *I'm* the one who catches it usually."

"So why don't you leave her?"

"Well that's what I am doing. Good grief, I've no idea why I'm telling you all this. You must think me a dreadful bore. Any sign of that snowplough yet?"

He glanced towards the nearest window, but the room was now swimming in what felt like a narcotic haze. When he finally focussed on its mullioned panes, all he saw was the snow plastering their exterior, and beyond that, billions of flakes tumbling on the wind.

"As I said before," Phoebe replied, "it may not come at all."

Arthur made no answer to that. Instead, he took another drink, only to find that his goblet was empty. He fumbled with the silver teapot, but that was empty as well.

"You've been astonishingly kind to us," he said. "If someone put my wife in the position I've put you in tonight, they wouldn't have got past the door. Not that she's unkind, mind. She *can* be kind, she can be very nice

… but if things aren't exactly the way she wants them, well …" He waggled his hand, as if that made everything clear.

"You're dry," Phoebe said, standing. "Can I get you another?"

"I'd better not. I won't be in a fit state to drive."

She took his goblet anyway. "One thing you're definitely not likely to meet up here is a policeman."

"That I can believe. Never one around when you need him."

She breezed away. Arthur laid back his head, wanting to close his eyes, but then felt Gabby plucking at his sleeve.

"Daddy, are we going yet?"

"We've only just arrived."

"We haven't only just arrived, we've been here for ages."

"We can't walk out now. This lady's been very nice to us."

"But we don't even know her." The child looked troubled. "And you're telling her lots of things about Mummy and you. Things you shouldn't be saying."

"She's never likely to meet us again, so what does it matter?"

"Can't we just go?"

"No we can't."

"I don't like it here." A whine had crept into her voice.

"Why? It's warm, it's cosy …"

"It feels wrong. We should be out there, trying to find our way to Aunt Lucy's."

But now Phoebe had returned. "Gabby, here's someone you might want to play with."

In her arms she held a small animal. At first Arthur was bamboozled. It looked like a bundle of pink fluff with a pair of big, long-lashed eyes. But then he realised that it was a poodle, a very young one. Gabby squealed in delight. Phoebe placed the animal down. Without any hesitation, it trotted across the room and allowed the little girl to pet it.

"Her name's Pupperkin," Phoebe said. "Take her over by the fire. That's where she likes it best."

"Come on, Pupperkin," Gabby cooed, backtracking over there.

The puppy followed obediently. Arthur stared at it. He'd seen some preposterous looking dogs in his time, but this took the biscuit. It had been dyed and coiffed absurdly. It was like a great pink puffball on legs – legs that had been completely shaven so that they looked like jointed spindles. Still, it seemed friendly enough. Its tail, which had also been shaven, apart from a great globe of fur at the end, wagged contentedly as Gabby sat down and began to cuddle it.

"Children are so delightfully easy to distract," Phoebe said.

Arthur nodded sagely. Then started talking about Moira again.

Perhaps it was just that he was drunk, which didn't happen very often these days without him getting scolded. Or maybe because he at last felt safe enough to unload all the hurt and resentment that he'd accrued over the years without fear of it leaking back to she-who-must-be-obeyed. Either way, it was an immense relief to get it all off his chest: the way Moira relentlessly put him down; the way she criticised his every opinion; the way nothing was ever good enough – seats on trains or aeroplanes, restaurant tables, holiday destinations – and how, almost invariably, the reason for this was because *he'd* been the one who'd booked. Of course, he wasn't solely in the firing line. No-one was spared Moira's vicious tongue: taxi drivers, hoteliers, shop assistants, receptionists, bank clerks, delivery boys, gardeners, mechanics, and anyone at all – no matter how dignified their position – from within the pyramid of underlings in her business life. Of course, even this was a source of woe for Arthur, because it was agonisingly embarrassing for him to have to stand and watch helplessly as she made fuss after fuss, only able to shrug when the rebuked person finally turned their humbled gaze upon him.

"You're clearly wasted on a woman like her, Arthur," Phoebe said, pouring him another goblet of tea. "I don't care what you say, you *are* a hero. If for no other reason than putting up with so much malice from one you love. This woman's obviously your Morgana, not your Guinevere. And that's all wrong.

"If I deserved better, Phoebe, I'd have got it by now. I'm a waster."

"You've been held back, that's all. You should break free."

He took another drink, well aware that it was slowing him down, making his thoughts sluggish. "Even if I did, what does the world hold for me now? I'm in my forties, for Christ's sake! Sorry, I don't normally swear …"

"Don't worry, that term doesn't offend me."

He glanced round at her, realising for the first time that she was sitting alongside him. Her legs were crossed and her robe had opened, revealing a flawless expanse of smooth, creamy thigh. She looked at him intently. This close, her eyes were dazzling blue pools, deep and mystical.

"And I don't agree that you're finished, either," she said softly. "There are many ways that a man like you can be found useful. But you've got to *want* it. You have to put yourself forward voluntarily. Do you understand what I mean?"

"I want it all right," he said.

"You do?" She seemed remarkably pleased.

"Well," and once again, so typically of him, Arthur dithered. "Well … actually, I'm not really sure what I want, if I'm honest."

"I see."

Sensing that he'd somehow disappointed her, he struggled to explain. "Obviously I'd like a new life. There's no denying that. It's just that … well, I can't see it happening."

"The question is not will it happen, but do you *want* it to happen?"

"I, erm …" He took another sip of his drink, which now seemed a lot cooler. "I'm half and half."

"Half and half?" By the expression on her face, the mere notion of that was repugnant to her.

"Yes."

"And that's your final word?"

"Well … yes, I'm afraid so."

There was a sudden yelp of pain, and Gabby leapt to her feet.

"She's just bitten me," she cried tearfully. She was grasping a finger on her left hand. "Pupperkin's just bitten me."

"Oh dear," Phoebe said. "That's unusual." She rose to her feet and scooped the dog into her arms. "I'll put her out of the way."

"Wha … what's that?" Arthur said. "The dog's bitten you?"

"Yes, look." Gabby crossed the room towards him, her face written with distress.

He leaned forward, only for his knees to buckle. He fell heavily to the floor, where the wind was driven out of him.

"Daddy, are you all right?" Gabby didn't so much sound shocked now as frightened. "Daddy, what's the matter?"

"Dunno …" And he genuinely didn't. The room was spinning. He tried to slither forward, but the mere act of crawling hand over hand left him fuddled and confused.

And then there was a bright light in the room.

"Someone's here!" Gabby yelled.

"What's … who?" With painful slowness, he turned his head to look at her. She was bouncing around animatedly. "Wh … what?"

"I said there's someone here!"

Groggily, he looked the other way. There was now no sign of their hostess or her wretched dog. Neither, for that matter, was there any sign of an internal door through which she might have exited. As he peered around, he flopped over onto his back; he really *was* intoxicated.

Gabby was edging out of his vision; she was moving towards the front door. "I'm going to get help," she said.

"No … wait," he stammered. "Tell Phoebe."

"I don't want to tell Phoebe. There's someone outside and I'm going to get them."

"Gabby …"

But she'd already gone. Yet to where? To whom?

Crazy as it might seem, Arthur had a nagging, nightmarish horror that it might be Moira out there. He rolled back onto his front and tried to get to all fours. "Ph-Phoebe?"

There was no response – no sound from anywhere else in the house. Then he heard voices outside. The front door had been opened, and he could hear them through breaks in the wind.

"You must help us," Gabby pleaded.

"Which way did he go?" a man replied.

"He's in there. You've got to help."

"I've looked in there, love. It's empty."

"Not the car."

"Gabby!" Arthur called. The thought that she was out on this isolated road, in the company of some man she didn't know spurred him to greater efforts. Once again the room swam, but he reached out and found the edge of the table. Propping himself against it, he clambered drowsily to his feet. The wind dropped again.

"But I don't want to go without him," Gabby was saying.

"I can't leave you here on your own."

"Mummy told me never to get lifts off strange men."

"I understand that, but you stay here and you're going to die."

"What about my Daddy?"

"There's nothing I can do about that now."

"Gabby …"

Arthur slurred as he stumbled across the lounge towards the top of the stair. The trip down it was almost a catastrophe. He swayed wildly, several times nearly losing his footing. But by some miracle he made it into the hall, and then he could see the open door ahead. The wind struck him in the face as he approached. After the warmth of the house, it was horrifically cold – like being slapped with a bucket of iced water. It revived him a little.

"Gabby?" He was now walking quickly, more steadily. He reached the door and could still hear her voice; she was down on the road.

"I don't want to … I don't want to get in."

"Darling, there's nothing else for it. Your dad should never have left you here."

Arthur blundered to the top of the steps. A large vehicle was parked below him, a yellow beacon revolving on top of it, its snow-plastered outline juddering to the vibrations of its mighty engine. An arcing steel blade at the front revealed it to be the aforementioned snowplough. On the roof of its driving-cab there was a powerful spotlight, and this was trained on the road ahead. But by the lesser light inside the cab, Arthur could see Gabby. She'd been placed in the passenger seat, where she was crying and struggling with her seatbelt. In the driver's seat, now closing his door, there was a man in a blue, quilted jacket, wearing a blue peaked cap. He took his gloves off and spoke into a radio hand-set.

Relieved that it was nothing more sinister, Arthur hobbled down the steps. "It's okay! I'm here! I'm her father!"

The man didn't hear, and it was hardly surprising. The wind wailed around them. Snowflakes slanted past like arrows. Arthur circled his own car, which was now almost completely buried apart from the driver's door; someone had obviously cleared that in order to peek through.

"I'm here!" he shouted again.

With a *thunk*, the snowplough driver changed gear. The engine revved.

"Hey!" Arthur staggered forward. "Wait a minute!"

As though in response to this, but more likely in response to Gabby – who was still visibly berating him – the snowplough man made no attempt to drive away yet, but operated some controls in front of him, and the spotlight on the roof began to swivel. Its brilliant beam penetrated a considerable distance even into murk like this, so it was with massive relief that Arthur felt it catch him in its full glare.

He advanced, waving a hand. However, there was no sudden opening of doors, no wild shouting of "Daddy, Daddy!" Puzzled, he shielded his eyes. From what he could see, both Gabby and the driver were peering straight at him, but neither was reacting. Gabby, who'd stopped crying briefly, merely looked worried. The driver, a grizzled old-timer, looked as though he felt he was wasting valuable time. The spotlight moved on, roving clear across the road and onto the bleak tundra beyond.

Arthur chased it round, but it was a struggle to catch up. With great effort, he got into it again, and again. But at no stage did either person in the cab seem to notice him. And now, finally, he saw that the driver was working the steering wheel.

"Hey!" Arthur scrambled forward, but immediately had to back up as the vehicle shifted on its axis, its blade only just missing him.

Slowly and ponderously it pulled a three-point turn. At one stage, Gabby was staring miserably down through her side-window. Right at him, right into his face. But though he shouted and waved frantically, she didn't so much as flinch.

"What the devil are you playing at?" Arthur screamed, his anguish and bemusement, and of course the gnawing chill, finally fuelling an uncharacteristic rage. "Stop this fucking crate!"

But the snowplough now faced back down the mountain road. It rumbled loudly, foul fumes exhaling from its rear pipes.

"Stop!" he shrieked. But it was no use.

With slow disbelief, he watched the vehicle lurch heavily forward, and in less than ten seconds vanish into the blizzard. The roar of its engine lasted a little longer, but very quickly that too was gone.

Arthur would have liked to remain there, shouting and cursing, and then probably shedding tears in his bewilderment. But likely as not those tears would freeze on his cheeks. Now that he'd been outside for a few minutes, he was feeling a cold the like of which he'd never known. Snowflakes lashed him; his fingers were already unbearably numb. All questions could be answered in due course. In the meantime, he needed to get warm again. He crossed the road, looking back up towards the house.

And he might as well have been struck by a sledge-hammer.

It was no longer there.

Above him – and, more importantly, above his car, which had not been moved one inch since he'd first arrived here – there was nothing but an icy ridge, fresh snow sheeting off it in the gale. Arthur gazed mutely upward. He blinked, shook his head, then staggered a few yards along the road in either direction, in case he'd got turned around while chasing the snowplough. But still there was nothing.

He was alone here, he gradually realised. Just him and the hillside, and the raw winter wind, which blew right through him – literally right *through* him.

THE MUMMERS

Of the dreadful events at Holker Hall …

Hugh Holker completed work on his great residence, Holker Hall, in 1793. It was a magnificent palace befitting any scene of rural splendour, but by origin Holker was not landed gentry. He came from a family of industrialists who attained wealth through the produce of their coal mines and cotton mills, which dotted the landscape thereabouts.

For all his extravagance, Holker was not held to be a tyrant but a philanthropist, who believed in doing right by those in his charge. In consequence, he built clean, decent dwellings for his workers, and planted the spectacular Groves, some 300 acres of verdant woodland, which encircled his property and were opened for public recreation in the summer of 1801.

Holker's main rival in the Bradleigh district was James Dangerfield, who had also made his fortune in coal and cotton. By 1801, Dangerfield's mills dominated the skylines of nearby Wigan, Bolton and Preston, and on several occasions he attempted to buy Holker's concerns.

Holker refused each offer, but James Dangerfield was no man to be denied. In an era when many boroughs were rotten, and swindle and corruption rife, the use of underhand methods was the rule. When it became clear that Holker would not sell, Dangerfield engineered sabotage and then intimidation. Agitators were employed to stir dissent among Holker's workforce, and highwaymen hired to perform payroll robberies so that his employees would not receive their wages on time. Holker held out resolutely, but the fatal blow fell on the Christmas Eve of 1804.

It was Holker's custom to have friends and relatives at the hall for the festive season. All manner of Yuletide revelry went on; carols were sung, there were parlour games, and much fine food was eaten. There were also Christmas mummers. These popular folklorists would prance to the hall in gay procession, arriving just before midnight. Once admitted, they would entertain the guests with a village dance, which though pagan in origin, had been adapted for the Christian feast. However, on the Christmas Eve of 1804, these mummers were waylaid in the Groves by James Dangerfield's ruffians. They were beaten, stripped of their costumes and bound naked to trees. The ruffians dressed themselves in the seasonal regalia and proceeded to Holker Hall incognito. Once admitted, they flew into a berserk rage, attacking the furniture and hangings with their ceremonial swords, and terrifying and driving out the guests. With the happy company dispersed, the villains fled, no doubt to some dissolute tavern to congratulate themselves. They neglected to consider the real mummers, still bound and naked in the icy forest. It was late on Christmas Day before these wretched souls were discovered. Hugh Holker's chief gamekeeper came upon them quite by accident. All were dead, having slowly frozen over a period of many hours.

The disaster sounded a death-knell for both James Dangerfield and Hugh Holker. Though Dangerfield was never brought to trial for his role in the affair, he was strongly implicated, and the scandal ruined his name. Holker, on the other hand, continued to live at Holker Hall, now a reclusive figure, but twelve months later was dead, having slipped on his own cellar stairs. Other deaths in his household followed shortly, a beloved nephew succumbing to pneumonia, an under-butler dying with a stroke. Rumours spread that Holker Hall was afflicted by a curse. A ghastly vision, it was said, manifested in the banquet lounge on the Christmas Eve of 1805, phantom figures performing a ritual dance of death ... the mummers' ghosts returning for vengeance exactly a year to the day after their cruel murder.

Belief still holds that every Christmas Eve, on the stroke of midnight, the spectral mummers return to Holker Hall to perform their pagan ritual, and that any individual luckless enough to witness this will die in the very near future.

Tales and Traditions of Old Lancashire, Vol. III

A vintage December afternoon. The sky a crisp pebble blue. The woods a silver tracery of frosted twigs. The forest floor still and silent under a thin carpet of dry, freshly-powdered snow.

Ordinarily, Phil would have been delighted. Even at thirty, he loved Christmas with a child's enthusiasm, though this year the outlook was a little gloomier. Let it snow, he reflected, let the sleigh-bells jingle, the candles ruddily smear the shop windows. Let all the family come around, for once full of genuine festive cheer. But it wouldn't make a lot of difference. For the first time in his working life, the hopes and fears of all Phil Stewart's years seemed to be coming to an end. Mind you, it wasn't as if his fate had been taken entirely out of his own hands. There were still things he could do. Well, there was *one* thing he could do. And that was why he was here, at Holker Hall, on a Christmas Eve afternoon.

He turned from the large fireplace, where holly logs crackled in a merry blaze, and took another sip of whiskey. It was finest malt and spilled over his tongue like sweet ash. Not that he was in the most receptive mood for something so exquisite. Phil glanced up as Eric Hazelwood, his former editor, came shuddering into the room. A spot of red glowed on each of Eric's wizened cheeks. Even with his duffle coat over his sweater, he looked frozen to the bone, and strode hurriedly to the fire to warm his hands.

"The van's in the second garage across the courtyard," Eric said.

Phil nodded.

Eric handed over the ignition key.

Phil stared at it as if it was infectious. A simple piece of ironmongery; yet so much now rode on it. "We're er … we're leaving at quarter-to-midnight, yeah?"

Eric nodded and made his way to the banquet table, where he poured himself a tot of malt.

"No earlier?" Phil wondered.

"Well … we don't want to give the game away."

Briefly, there was silence. Phil hadn't seen his ex-boss this dejected since the death of his wife ten years before. The guy was morose, a pale shadow of the once hearty figure who'd helmed the local weekly with such verve and good humour for so many happy, productive years.

“I suppose we’re doing the right thing?” Phil said.

Eric shrugged. “Dunno.”

“We can always cancel.”

“No chance,” Eric said. “No chance at all.” And he strode away again to make more checks.

Phil surveyed the enormous room. It was as ready as it could be. The banquet table was baronial in proportion, and laid with a feast fit for any king; not just the usual roast beef, egg sandwiches and vol-au-vents, but extra stuff, special stuff, real Christmas fare: a Norfolk turkey stuffed with sage and onion, medallions of venison with apple-slices, smoked salmon and truffles, chicken in port, quail’s eggs, oysters, sweet meats, gateaux, plum pudding and mince-pies with brandied pouring-cream. It had cost them a pretty penny, but it would be worth it for the occasion. A similar amount had been spent on the décor: mistletoe adorned the lintels; great swags of evergreen brocaded the hearth. Against the north wall, a spruce fir was arrayed with streamers and fairy lights. There was also a bar of course, unmanned and free-of-charge; crates of beer were stacked behind it; bottles of spirit lined its shelves. Phil doubted the bar at Holker Hall had been so well stocked for many years, even though it had hosted larger functions than this.

These days, the old place was a typical council-owned stately home. Georgian by origin, it was a grandiose, red-brick affair, rambling in size and pleasant enough to look upon, though its exterior flattered to deceive, for inside there was much neglect. The majority of the rooms were empty and unfurnished, while one whole wing was so decrepit that it had been sealed off from the public. The Recreation and Amenities Committee had only ever perceived it as a place to rent out for weddings and christenings; they’d been charged with its maintenance since the late 1960s, and in all that time had never once considered the possibility of restoring the historic seat to its Regency grandeur. Such was the mentality of small-town administrators in the north of England. Were Holker Hall located in the Cotswolds or West Country, it would not only be filled with antiques and roped-off old masters by now, but waxen figures in Cromwellian guise would guard its doorways, there'd be flags and suits of armour, fêtes on bank holidays, and garden parties and jousts in high summer. As it was, set in a largely redundant coal-mining borough, Holker Hall was a folly, a curiosity. If it hadn't been for the Groves, which were still extensively enjoyed by local people, Phil was sure the building would long ago have been boarded up and left to rack and ruin.

He moved to the mullioned casement and gazed out. Wintry dusk was falling, a frozen mist rising between the black stanchions of the trees. The gravel drive, which wound for two miles through the Groves and finally joined Bradleigh Lane via a gigantic pair of Victorian wrought-iron gates, was icy and glittering in the twilight. For the first time that day, there was a spooky aspect to the place. Suddenly, Phil wondered if this idea was workable or even sensible. On one hand, he hoped it was, and he hoped the pay-off would be dramatic – even though the ramifications would be terrifying. But on the other, he suspected he was being over-emotional, maybe even stupid.

Eric reappeared at his shoulder. "You don't need to stand sentry, you know. They'll be here when they're here."

"This is tantamount to murder," Phil said quietly.

"Only if you believe the stories."

"Eric, I've covered court cases where nightclub brawlers had bitten each other's noses and ears off. The trial of a father who'd deliberately drowned both his babies in the canal. I've been in cancer wards, hospices. I've spoken to the homeless, the drug-addicted. What I'm saying is … I've been around, I'm hard-headed. And yet here I am, involved in something like this."

"Know what you mean." Eric shrugged. "But what's that famous phrase, there're more things in Heaven and Earth …"

"I've always been open-minded, Eric. It's just that now I'm wishing I wasn't."

Eric chuckled. "Catholic guilt, mate. Not as if you're pulling a trigger, is it?"

"Then why are we doing this?"

"Let's call it an experiment."

"An experiment?"

"Yeah." Eric grinned, cold and hard. "And, personally, I can't wait for the result. Now, you speak to the WPO?"

Phil nodded. Joe Morley, the borough's Woodlands Project Officer, had been a good contact of his throughout his years in the local press; their relationship had now reached a stage where neither of them asked questions if the other wanted a favour. In consequence, Joe had assured Phil that the gates to the Holker estate would be open on time this evening, and that once events got under way there'd be no Parks Department patrols to disturb anyone.

Phil wasn't sure whether to be pleased about that, or unnerved.

*

Several hours later, two taxis arrived, skating to a halt on the slippery gravel.

Phil waited at the window. He was dressed up and preened by now and, to calm himself down, had drunk a little more than he perhaps should have, but his nervousness increased as various swaggering figures disgorged from the vehicles. They were already talking loudly, cackling in their normal obnoxious way. No doubt they'd had a tipple or two in the pub beforehand – at Al's expense. Al, or rather Al Green, was new editor-in-chief of the *Chronicle & Mercury*. The guy was easy to recognise by his snide chuckle. Again, Phil found himself unable to believe that this young lout had replaced the intellectual Eric Hazelwood in the newspaper's head chair.

"Better let them in, I suppose," Eric said, rising from an armchair. He'd changed into a suit and tie, but as usual – thanks to his gruff northern disposition, thick grey hair and lanky frame – looked awkward and scruffy. "They're early, but what can we expect when there's free booze and food?"

Phil glanced back through the window. His lip curled.

Al Green: thirty-eight years old and the archetypical wideboy. Broad-shouldered and bullish, with a spiked flat-top and permanent sneer, he even looked the part. Years of pushing and shoving his way up whichever ladder he'd decided to take his chances on, hadn't moderated his guttural Salford brogue one iota, or his aggressively domineering attitude. Such was his anticipation of personal success that top-dog was the only position he'd ever accept; lack of qualification or credential never bothered him. With such confidence, you'd have thought his background public school rather than Manchester comprehensive, but this wasn't a mistake you'd make for long – not when he squared up to you, as he did if he thought you were posing even a tiny problem, and fixed you with a gaze that seemed to threaten actual violence.

Phil didn't think he'd ever hated anyone half as much.

Even as Green strutted in now, his smile didn't reach his steely eyes. As usual, his good ol' boy smarm was only paper-thin. Perhaps he already scented the trap.

"All right, Stewpot?" he said, unbuttoning his sheepskin coat. He knew Phil didn't like the nickname 'Stewpot', so he made sure to use it on every possible occasion, a heavy handed but effective ploy, very typical of the new regime at the *Chronicle & Mercury*.

Phil smiled and said nothing. Three months into Al Green's rule, he already knew that resistance was futile.

Things had first started going wrong four years earlier, when the *Bradleigh Mercury's* position as the town's leading newspaper was suddenly challenged by the launch of a new free-sheet, the *Bradleigh Chronicle*. For all that it was a regal publication with a long and honourable history, the *Mercury* was not geared up for a tough battle. In fifteen years of good but gentlemanly supervision, Eric Hazelwood had cultivated a civilised staff and a great family atmosphere. In short, with no rivals to speak of, they'd gone soft. Even though the *Chronicle*, which infamously paid dirt-cheap wages, utilising untrained school leavers rather than professionals, couldn't compete in the news stakes, it enjoyed one massive advantage: its advertising crew were able to tell potential clients that the *Chronicle* was delivered to two hundred thousand front doors every week. Even if many of these deliveries were promptly binned or left to gather dust in derelict hallways, it was still an impressive figure to quote compared to the sixty thousand the *Mercury* sold. Perhaps inevitably, a lion's share of the *Mercury's* clients thus switched their advertising to the *Chronicle*, and almost overnight the *Mercury* circulation shrank catastrophically. Within a few months, the grand old paper was selling less than thirty thousand copies.

Such decline could not be tolerated for long, and after three and a half years, Anderson's – the national newspaper group who owned the *Mercury* – took drastic action; they bought the *Chronicle* and merged the two titles into the *Bradleigh Mercury & Chronicle*. A sensible appreciation of difficult times perhaps; but not where the *Mercury's* staff were concerned. Employees could not be merged, so clearly there'd have to be redundancies, and as the majority of the *Mercury's* team were more experienced and therefore more expensive, it seemed likely they would take the brunt of it.

And they did.

In fact, it was a massacre. Phil was one of the very few survivors. Even Eric Hazelwood, the jewel in the *Mercury's* crown, was removed from his post to accommodate *Chronicle* boss Al Green, though to avoid tribunal, the older editor was shoved aside rather than cast onto the heap. They created a job for him: 'sub-editor on stone'. It sounded good, but it was actually on a much smaller wage and located *outside* his beloved newsroom. Overnight, it seemed, the *Mercury* world had ended. Not only were out-of-town strangers suddenly occupying the desks and occupying them in the triumphal way the Nazis had occupied Paris, but old trusts were immediately dispensed with and new customs introduced: sarcasm, bullying, eavesdropping.

"Happy Christmas, mate!"

Phil came back to his senses. Voices filled the vestibule; someone was talking to him.

"All the best!" bawled big Nick Curtis, pumping Phil's hand. "Well … Holker Hall on Christmas Eve, hey! What a cracking idea!"

"Oh … er, yeah. Happy Christmas, Nick." Phil did his best not to choke on the words.

Nick Curtis, until recently a cub reporter on the *Chronicle*, was now sports editor of the combined titles. He liked to model himself on Green, but even though a head taller, he lacked the presence, not to mention the acumen. Hardly an impressive back-up man, but a perfect lieutenant for someone like Green, who demanded loyalty over ability.

Right now, Curtis was following his primal instincts and, having unceremoniously dumped Phil, homed in on the bar. Others of his sort followed: Steve Benedict: twenty-three and already news editor; he always presented himself in sharp suits, but only ever succeeded in looking like an Easter leaver attending his first interview; chief sub Barbara Banks, a foursquare, brutal-looking woman who browbeat her juniors, but in the company of fellow middle management, adopted the ladette approach, effing and blinding, chain-smoking and sinking pints; feature writer Elaine Blythe, totally minus talent, but sexy in an elfin sort of way, and currently having an affair with married man Green. There were several others, whose names alone irritated Phil: soccer pundit Mike Scanty, crime reporter Jim Church, women's editor Yvonne Chantelle; every one of them useless, yet still a legend in his or her own mind.

"Hey, Stewpot … I always thought Holker Hall was unavailable in December?"

Phil glanced round. It was Green. Again, those penetrating eyes, as if he knew much more than he was letting on. Briefly, Phil was lost for words. Then, mercifully, Eric cut in.

"We asked, we got," he said simply.

Green considered this and shrugged. "Well … great! Superb idea." Predictably, he wasn't entirely satisfied. "Just out of interest, where's the money coming from?"

He'd phrased it as a friendly question, but Phil knew that in reality he was checking that nothing owed from his own entertainments budget.

"It's all on us," Eric assured him. "From the old *Mercury* staff to our new friends on the *Chronicle.* You've shown us the way. Can't argue with profit margins like yours."

"Very generous of you," Green replied slowly, as if he couldn't quite believe this. "Well … I suppose we'd better get stuck in. Come on folks, *it's Christmas!*"

Suddenly he was jovial again, magnanimous even, as if this was something *he'd* organised. As one, his crowd waded into the feast. Phil still thought eight of them too few, but Eric had opted not to invite the vast bulk of the *Chronicle* staff as its reporters and subs were little more than menials on micro-wages who only thought they were real journalists because Al Green told them they were. "No," he'd said, "disposing of their officers" would be sufficient.

"We got any music, Stewpot?" Green shouted.

"Yeah, course," Phil replied. "Just a mo …"

"Al!" Barbara Banks brayed from the other end of the table. "Try these oysters, they're fantastic!"

"Oh, Al," said Elaine Blythe in near-orgasmic tones, "these truffles are just Heaven!"

Unable to bear the soft-soaping any longer, Phil was grateful to slide into the adjoining cloakroom, where spare boxes of booze were waiting and a pile of DJ gear occupied one of the walls, including a large if slightly old-fashioned music centre. He slipped a Christmas hits tape into it and pressed 'play'. Perry Como came on, smoothly crooning *God Rest Ye Merry, Gentlemen.*

It was always "Al this, Al that", Phil thought. They were so obvious, these people. Yet not only was it tolerated, it was rewarded. How superficial could you be? It was like the court of some medieval king.

Speaking of which …

Phil glanced at a gilt-framed portrait propped in a corner. It was done in dark oils and had been varnished in order to preserve it. Much of the varnish was now dirty and yellowed, but through it the deeply troubled visage of Hugh Holker was still visible: an elderly man with sagging jowls, a heavily furrowed brow and thick grey tufts for sideburns. Phil had been in to look at the picture several times already, and still found it compelling. The artist had depicted Holker leaning on his fist in a posture of dignified contemplation but had etched despair and even fear into the final composition. The old industrialist's eyes bore a stark quality, as if some ghastly apparition had just materialised before him. In the background meanwhile there were indistinct mist-forms, swirls and eddies of smoke or fog, which might have had more to do with the picture's age than the artist's intent, but which were ominously obscure all the same.

"… to save us all from Satan's power when we were gone astray," sang Perry.

With a pang of unease, Phil was reminded of his purpose here. He glanced at his watch. It read seven-thirty; time was ticking away quickly. Almost too quickly. He shivered. Trepidation, anxiety, fear, all mixed in one; but then he heard again the raucous, gluttonous shouts filling the room behind him, and his nerves settled.

What was it Eric had said? That this was an experiment?

Yes, and Phil too was keen to see the result.

He went back into the banquet lounge, which was already filling up with cigarette smoke and smelled of beer. He looked around: Nick Curtis had latched onto Eric and was boring him to death with football talk. Not far to their right, Steve Benedict was buttering up Green. "I kept saying to him," Benedict bragged, "no-one knows how to party like journos. I says to him, the average journo's breakfast is a pint of lager and a cigarette …" This was Steve Benedict, twenty-three.

Phil moved to the banquet table, where the women had nailed themselves. Barbara Banks, smoking and eating at the same time with remarkable dexterity, was querying certain items of food. "I've always wondered what sweetmeat is," she said to Elaine Blythe. She craned her bullneck round. "Eric … what's sweetmeat?"

Eric, grateful for the distraction, broke away from Curtis. "It's like cake or sweet bread. You normally have it with a savoury dish."

Phil wanted to laugh when he heard Elaine Blythe quietly ask: "What's a savoury dish?"

Eric sidled up to him. "Kids in a candy shop," he mumbled.

Phil snorted quietly. "They've been kids in a candy shop for the last three months. No-one suspects anything, I take it?"

Eric chuckled. "Be honest, would you expect this lot to know the history of any prominent building in Bradleigh?"

Phil pondered. For once, the dipsticks' complete lack of knowledge about the town they'd appointed themselves to be the voice of was working against them. That was nice.

"Seems they've booked their taxis home for half-twelve," Eric added. "That could be the longest half-hour they've ever had."

"I hope so," Phil replied. "Lord … I hope so."

*

It was Eric Hazelwood who'd first told Phil about the mummers of Holker Hall.

This had been several years before, in the halcyon days when the *Mercury* had been the plain old *Mercury*. At the time, they were discussing a possible centrespread on local ghosts. Eric had long been a student of the supernatural, but he wasn't keen on using the Holker Hall mystery. After all, this wasn't some spectral pussy cat with a cute purr, or a thirsty pub ghost who drew himself generous measures after hours and in so doing helped drum up custom. There was little to snigger at in this tale, and those members of the Bradleigh public who knew about it responded accordingly. The myth wasn't known widely enough for the hall to be shunned; the Groves still played host to adventurous children and picnicking families, especially in summer, while the ornate old building was a source of architectural interest, but that was about it. Few went near the place at night, and none on Christmas Eve. These spooks didn't just scare you;

they signed your death warrant. It was only a story of course, but why take the chance?

Phil still wasn't sure if he believed it, though now, as eight o'clock came and went, then nine and finally ten, he was increasingly distracted from the drunken frolics in the banquet lounge to the opaque winter darkness outside. He could well imagine the miles and miles of frozen, unlit woodland lying between himself and civilisation. Once or twice, he thought vague forms were cavorting out there, though that was unlikely. It was way too early yet; the mummers were only supposed to emerge from the Groves at midnight. Of course, no-one could say for sure, because allegedly no-one had lived to tell.

Behind him, Eric, who'd loosened up as the party had worn on, was entering into a little mischief. Phil was half-listening to a jovial conversation he was engaged in about weird and wonderful Christmas customs, when it struck him that his old friend was deliberately steering things towards the darker, more pagan tradition.

"Mumming, of course, was another thing," Eric said.

"Mumming?" a few of them echoed.

"Yeah. Never heard of mumming?"

There were blank expressions all round. Phil sipped his beer and watched with interest.

"Mummers were entertainers who would come into the big country houses on Christmas Eve and perform for the guests," Eric explained. "They were mime dancers, who'd act out a popular Christmas story."

"Panto season," Barbara Banks said profoundly. Then she belched.

"Sort of," Eric replied. "By the nineteenth century, mumming had become a kind of clowning affair. The miracle plays had gone over to Dick Whittington and stuff like that. But the custom goes back to pre-Christian times. It's like a lot of the stuff we have at Christmas. It was all about regeneration … the death and rebirth of the natural year. The mummers would dress up in greenery, with odd masks on, usually animal faces. Sometimes they'd even have swords, and they'd finish with a sword-dance, which would culminate in a pretend beheading."

"Really?" Elaine Blythe said wide-eyed, realising she'd discovered something she could turn into a feature this time next year. If only, she thought, there was some history for it locally.

Eric nodded. "It signified they were killing off the old year. Sort of sacrificing it, so it could be replaced by something better."

Phil glanced at Al Green. The bastard was never interested in anything Eric had to say. The fact the older guy was still on the company payroll riled him enormously. Now, he was staring vacantly, his casual body language suggesting he didn't care two hoots about mummers or mumming. Phil wondered what Green's body language would suggest at one minute past twelve.

"Give me Dick Whittington any time," Barbara Banks said, cracking another can. "Hey … you should've seen the legs on the lad they had playing him at St. Hugh's last year."

There were gales of ribald laughter.

"That was a girl, wasn't it!" Steve Benedict said.

Barbara took a slurp of beer. "Had a fair old lunchbox in her tights, if she was."

There was more laughter. The alcohol flowed again.

Eric sidled up to Phil. "And a good time was had by all."

"Almost seems a shame."

"Not going soft on me, I hope?"

“They nearly seem human in this environment,” Phil quietly replied.

“This environment comes around once a year. Remember what they’re like the rest of the time.”

Phil glanced at the clock. “It’s almost eleven. We’ve got half an hour.”

Eric nodded. “When you leave, remember to take the van up the dirt road to the north exit.”

Phil looked curiously round. “What do you mean when *I* leave? Eric … you’re not thinking of doing something stupid? Like staying?”

Eric gave him a frank stare. “Tell the truth … I’ve been thinking of nothing else.”

“Damn it, Eric!” Phil found difficulty keeping his voice down. He ushered his old friend away from the others. “What’s all this about now?”

“Phil, it’s just a legend. We don’t know for a *fact* that something’s going to happen.” Eric paused. “The best we can really hope for is they get the fright of their lives. And … well, I want to be here to see it.”

“Excuse me, but that’s bollocks! You want to be here because you’ve had enough. Because you want to pop your clogs with the rest of them. I’m not impressed! I can understand you’re pissed off, but you got chucked out because our company’s full of shallow bastards who know nothing about newspapers. It’s no reflection on your ability.”

“I’m fifty-eight, Phil … what future have I got in any business now?”

“The same one you had before, *if* we get Green out of the way! Look … Eric, once he’s gone, they’ll need someone who knows what they’re doing just to take up the slack.”

“Hardly a glorious end to my career.”

"Oh Jesus, spare me! Look ..." Phil stuck his hand into his pocket and dragged out the key to the van. "I want *you* to hold this."

Eric gazed at it but made no move to accept.

"Because I'm not going without you," Phil added.

Eric glanced at the clock; it read eleven-o-five. "Time's running out, mate."

Phil was acutely aware of this: the minutes ticking steadily away; the tension coiling inside him. Defiantly, he slammed the key on the table. Almost on cue, the music halted. There were groans and expletives from the *Chronicle* staff, some of whom had started to drunkenly dance. Nick Curtis was giving it the old air-guitar.

"I'll change the record," Eric said loudly, strolling away from the key.

Phil glanced sideways – and saw Al Green watching with interest, as if he'd witnessed everything that had just gone on. Phil felt like chucking him a V-sign but opted instead to grin and wipe some imaginary sweat from his brow. Then he followed Eric, who was kneeling by the music-centre when Phil entered the cloak room.

"You've been planning this for ages, haven't you?" Phil said. "I wondered why you were so keen. I mean ... when I first suggested it, I was only joking."

Eric slid another tape into the machine. "You must admit, it's an unusual form of suicide."

"There's no guarantee it'll be painless."

Eric shrugged and stood up. In the background, the tidy acoustics of Greg Lake's *I Believe in Father Christmas* filled the air. Phil glanced at his watch. Time seemed to be spinning on at phenomenal pace. It had already gone from 11.05 to 11.20.

"This is something you youngsters will never understand, Phil," Eric said. "About leaving your mark, having the last word. You know me, I've never been precious about my work. But this goes deeper than that. Much deeper. I mean, I really … *really* want to be here when Al Green and his imposters get what's coming to them. I want to *see* it. More importantly, I want to be able to tell them *I'm* the one responsible."

"And what if nothing happens?"

"Then nothing's lost."

Elaine Blythe blundered in, giggling, hair loose and straggly. Nick Curtis came barging behind her, clasping a sprig of mistletoe. "'Scuse us, folks!" he bellowed, rampaging round the room, scattering odds and ends.

When they'd gone, Eric made to follow them. "Best get on, Phil. You'll be late."

"Eric …"

But Eric had vanished back into to the banquet lounge. As he entered, he made a grand announcement: "Sorry everyone, but Phil Stewart's got to shoot. Bit of a shame, but apparently he's meeting a young lady."

Phil came in one second too late to prevent this and could only stand there unable to respond. One by one, Green and his crowd turned, new expressions on their red, sweaty faces. As if by magic, Eric produced his coat for him.

"Don't let us detain you, Stewpot," Green said, grinning.

"Er … right," Phil stammered.

"Anyone we know, Philip?" Yvonne asked.

"Er, no."

He found himself being helped on with his jacket. He tried to say something else, to tell them he'd changed his mind, but Eric stepped into his line of vision. "See you, mate."

Phil wanted to argue, to insist that his friend come with him – but how could he? He was shuffled purposefully towards the door, hands clapping his shoulders, shouts of "Happy Christmas!" ringing in his ears.

"Be good when you meet her, Phil, love," roared Barbara Banks, planting a smoke and oyster-scented kiss on his cheek. "But if you can't be good, be superb!"

There were more brazen laughs, more best wishes. Beyond them, Phil saw Eric standing by the table, frozen in time, a wax effigy rather than a man. Then he was out in the vestibule, being hustled along, people telling him he had to be there to give her the first Christmas kiss, hopefully the first of many. It was at least twenty yards long, that vestibule, but Phil was down it before he knew what was happening and standing beside the front door, which Steve Benedict had opened for him. Still they encouraged him, congratulated him. And now the outside air flowed in, bitingly cold. Someone gave a melodramatic shudder.

"See you, Stewpot!" one of them shouted. "Have a great Christmas … ta-ra!"

Phil nodded, shook hands, and then was stepping outside under the great marble portico. And the door was closing at his back … with a thump.

There was silence.

In some heavyweight drama, Phil might have stood there for ages, pondering, regretting lost opportunities. This was reality though, and reality was well below zero. He hugged himself, his breath pluming in thick clouds. He glanced towards the Groves; they were black as anthracite, dense, twisted, yet in the glacial starlight snowy pathways were visible penetrating to their tangled depths. Phil wondered what time it was. Was he about to spy movement down there; odd, misshapen things capering clumsily among the trees, drawing steadily closer, perhaps to the rhythmic beating of a drum?

Shivering at the thought, he turned and set off along the side-path that led around the building to the garages at the rear. It was no quick journey. Corner followed corner, wing followed wing; he passed snowy lawns and dead, frozen flowerbeds – and then he remembered that he didn't have the van's key. He halted mid-stride, slapping at his pocket just to be sure. But it wasn't there. Obviously it wasn't. In his mind's eye, he could still picture the blasted thing lying on the tablecloth in the banquet lounge.

Phil glanced back along the path, swearing under his breath.

It wouldn't be easy going inside again. He'd have to explain, and people would say he shouldn't drive after drinking, a point he'd have to argue. And of course, then he'd be back in Eric's orbit. He'd be tempted once more to try and take the guy with him, to come up with any excuse he could to get him outside, where, if necessary, he could *force* him into the vehicle. Maybe that was the solution.

Phil started back, even more conscious now that time was ticking away. He started to run, only closely avoiding slipping on several occasions. The trick was not to look at the Groves, he told himself as he arrived back at the front, not under any circumstances. According to myth, you couldn't risk so much as a glimpse. Eyes locked on the path in front, he strode back under the portico and lifted the heavy brass knocker. Behind him, he could sense the emptiness of the night. Assuming that it *was* empty. Because there was no point denying it now. *They'd* be on their way; they'd practically be here.

Phil's fist clenched on the knocker. Fear grew on him with extraordinary speed. He couldn't afford to waste a single second.

There was a loud *screech* behind him.

Directly behind him.

He whirled around, unconsciously releasing the knocker, which slammed against the wood, causing the door to creak open a few inches. Clearly, it hadn't been closed properly. Not that this mattered now, because suddenly and rather bewilderingly everyone was outside with him.

At least, it looked like everyone.

The screech had come from a set of tyres. The tyres belonged to the only vehicle at the hall: the van Phil and Eric had brought from the vehicle pool at work. Now that van sat chugging on the driveway, a huddle of shapes crammed into its rear section, riotous laughter sounding through its narrow, dust-smeared windows. In the frigid air, a fog of exhaust billowed around it.

Several seconds passed before Phil was able to approach. Had Eric had second thoughts? But even as he asked himself this, the driver's window wound down, to reveal not Eric Hazelwood but Al Green. Eric wasn't in the front passenger seat either; Elaine Blythe occupied that spot, swilling from a tin of lager. Phil's puzzlement turned slowly to prickling fear. A barnyard dirge of drunken mirth spilled out again from the rear of the vehicle; he couldn't imagine that Eric was installed in there either.

Green cut the engine and leaned out of the window. "Thanks for this, Stewpot." He held up the key. "Good of you to leave it where I could find it."

Phil was lost for words.

"Don't look so nonplussed," Green added. "We went out the back way. Much quicker than coming out round the front."

"What's … what's going on, Al?"

Green's smile became an insolent sneer. "I think you already know, pal. But in case you're wondering how *I* knew, thank your good mate, Dave Plumpton."

"Dave Plu …" Phil's words tailed off in disbelief.

Plumpton was a photographer back at the paper. Aside from Phil and Eric, he was the only other *Mercury* man whose job had survived the merger.

"Don't worry, he didn't grass you up," Green said. "I was just chatting to him, asked why he wasn't coming to the Christmas do. He let it slip he'd been told to stay away … by you."

Phil felt his stomach turn to water.

Green's smile hardened. "You may think I'm some Manc carrot-cruncher, Stewpot, and maybe compared to you bastards with your degrees and diplomas and what-not, I am, but what I've got is up *here*." He tapped his temple. "I've been one step ahead of you prats all the way, and I wasn't going to get caught out this time. Once I got a sniff you were up to something, it didn't take a lot of digging to find out what it was."

"Where's Eric, Al?" Phil tried to keep his voice steady, but it was difficult.

Green chuckled. "Fun idea, all the same … bit kooky, but fun. Be interesting to see how it works out for you two." He withdrew the key from sight, and the engine rumbled back to life. "Course … you'll not be in the office to tell us. Your notice of dismissal's on the mantelpiece inside."

"Where's Eric?" Phil's voice rose to a shout.

Green chuckled again. "You'll notice I've had it gift-wrapped."

There was further baying laughter from the rear of the van. Phil lurched forward and slammed a hand onto its roof. "I asked you where Eric was!"

"No need to get testy." Green knocked off the handbrake. "He's inside. Wasn't too impressed when I told him what I've just told you. Took a swing at me. I had to take one back."

Phil sucked in his breath.

"But never fear," Green added, "I've got seven witnesses in case it ever gets to court."

"Want to try a swing at *me?*" Phil shouted, kicking the door.

Green glanced at his watch. "Don't think I have to, Stewpot … it's almost twelve."

He winked and jammed his foot down. The van sped away, spewing ice and gravel behind it. Seconds later, it had vanished along the road into the Groves, a cheery but muffled chorus of *Jingle Bells* gradually fading into silence.

Phil charged inside the building, dashing along the vestibule and bursting into the banquet lounge. The first thing he saw was Eric Hazelwood lying prone among the streamers and dog-ends. Phil stumbled forward. The casualty was bloodied around the mouth and left temple, and clearly deeply unconscious. In one hand, he clasped a crumpled note, torn fragments of gift-paper still adhered to it. Similar paper was visible on the mantel; it was a sealed envelope propped against a candlestick. It bore the legend:

'Stewpot. Ex-employee'

"You bas … bastards!" Phil stuttered, falling to one knee.

He felt for a pulse at Eric's wrist; the flesh was fishy cold, not so much as a tremor of life. With growing panic, he placed his fingers on Eric's neck, searching for the carotid.

Still there was no response. He looked wildly around. Was there a phone? But before he could get up to search for one, a finger of ice touched his heart.

Because he'd just heard something.

A drum. A single drum. Playing at a steady rhythmic beat.

Phil froze where he knelt, ears straining. Definitely a drum. And it sounded as if it was approaching the house from somewhere outside.

... thud ... thud ... thud ... thud ...

There was something else too. Feet, several pairs of them, great heavy feet, shod possibly in clogs or hobnail boots, but clumping hard, banging out an intricate pattern on the gravel of the drive. To Phil's disbelief, he realised that he recognised the tune.

… oranges and lemons, say the bells of ...

He didn't need to glance at the clock to realise that it was exactly midnight. Even as this occurred to him, the timbre of the approaching tattoo altered. From 'clumping' to 'clattering'. Concrete – they'd reached the portico.

… five farthings, say the bells of St Martin's ...

Phil's hair stood slowly on end. An Arctic wind gushed into the building, doors swinging and slamming throughout the interior. The prisms of the chandeliers started to rattle, the candles to gutter, and then the electric lights to fade.

... when will you pay me, say the bells of Old …

With a thundering crash the front door was thrown open, and now those feet were in the vestibule, stamping the floorboards in a frenzied jig. It sounded as if there were a thousand of them.

… say the bells of Shoreditch …

The drum boomed; it was deafening. And only at this point did Phil's paralysis lapse, only now did the animal instinct of 'flee to survive' dash over him.

But where to? And what about Eric?

He looked around in a daze of terror, and then disbelief. For suddenly the room was hung with frozen cobwebs, everything in there – walls, ceiling, even Christmas decorations – smothered in frosted lace, though fiery red lace rather than white, for though the lights had died, the Yule logs in the hearth continued to blaze, casting writhing crimson phantasms from wall to wall.

… when will that be, say the bells of Stepney …

This transformation was so startling it almost distracted Phil from the peril of his position. But not for long; the door to this room was also swung open, and he threw himself down over Eric's body, screwing his eyes shut, clamping his hands across the back of his head.

... I'm sure I don't know ...

He knew he couldn't look. That was all Phil could do, he realised – not look.

...says the great bell ...

The feet were all around him, circling in a fury, hitting the floor with gunshot force.

... of Bow!

"No," Phil screamed, "no!"

There were swishings and swipings in the air above him. And he didn't need to guess what that was.

... chop ... chop ... chop ... chop ...

The tears froze to ice crystals in his eyes

... chop ... chop ...

Phil could no longer breathe.

... here comes a chopper ...

Was this it, then? Was this finally it?

... to chop off your ...

*

"By all accounts, you're lucky to be alive," the policeman said.

"I am?" Phil croaked.

He was still only vaguely aware of his surroundings. They'd brought him up from Intensive Care earlier that day. From what he could see, he was now in an ordinary side-ward, all curtains and white tiles, nurses bustling back and forth.

"Well, you were unconscious for nearly two days." The policeman was a heavy-set bloke, fat-necked and red-faced, the uniform bulging tightly on his frame. He seemed pleasant enough for all that, even if he was sitting beside Phil with his pen and notebook in hand. "And in sub-zero conditions. Looks like the hall's heating packed in for some reason. You're lucky Mr. Morley found you when he did."

"Good old Joe," Phil groaned. "He always comes through for me." And then, in a horrible rush, the memory of what happened also came through. "Eric!" Phil gasped, wanting to sit up but too weak. "Eric Hazelwood ... where is he?"

The policeman cleared his throat. "He's the one I want to speak to you about, actually."

"Oh no ... no, don't tell me he's ..."

"No, he's alive. But he's in a bad way."

“How bad?” Phil felt relief but also bemusement. What exactly was going on here?

“He’s in a coma. Seems he gave his head a crack on the corner of the dining table. It’s made of mahogany. Tough as concrete.”

“Is he going to be all right?”

“I’m afraid we don’t know … he sustained a fractured skull.”

“But he’s alive?”

“He’s alive, but …” The policeman paused, as if there was something on his mind. “Mr. Stewart, *this* is why I need to talk to you. How did it happen? Did you two have a fight or something?”

“*Us two?* No! No way … it was Green! It was that bastard Green who hit him!”

“Al Green?”

“Sounds like you know him?”

The policeman frowned. “I’m afraid so.”

“Why afraid?”

“I’m sorry to be the one to tell you, but … he’s dead.”

“Dead?” The word came out a whisper. Many times in recent months Phil had yearned to be given this very information, but now it left him stunned.

The policeman seemed irritated and uncomfortable both at the same time. “You haven’t already been told about this?”

Phil shook his head.

“I see. Well …” The policeman’s face reddened even more. “He died on Christmas Eve, on his way back from the party at Holker Hall. Nasty accident, I’m afraid. Drove his vehicle straight into the wrought-iron gates on Bradleigh Lane. From the post-mortem report, it seems he was drunk. Plus, the conditions were icy …”

"And he didn't know the gates would be closed," Phil added, almost to himself.

"Sorry?"

Phil tried to explain: "He must've thought the gates would be open … but Joe Morley said he'd be closing them, and that we'd have to leave the estate by the dirt road at the back."

"And Mr. Green wouldn't have known that?"

"Al wasn't supposed to be driving."

"Well .... I suppose that makes things a bit clearer."

"What about the others?" Phil asked.

The policeman went redder still, much redder. "Like I say, it was a nasty accident. The vehicle wasn't suited for carrying passengers. There were no seats in the back, never mind seatbelts. It was also pretty overcrowded … so, an impact like that … well, they didn't stand a chance."

"J … Jesus," Phil stammered.

"I'm sorry."

But Phil was no longer listening. Inside his head there was turmoil: not just guilt, but dismay, disbelief. Had Green and his team spotted the mummers after all? Had the spectres emerged from the trees just as the van roared past? Or had it simply been an accident? A plain old accident? Phil had some vague recollection of the weird events before he'd lost consciousness, but nothing clear – a nightmare maybe, fuelled by the mythology of that place. So yes, an accident. Surely no more than that.

"At least they didn't all go as badly as your Mr. Green," the policeman added in a subdued tone.

Phil glanced up, confused.

"I'm sorry to say that he was thrown clean through the windscreen." The policeman's eyes roved the floor. "He was … he was decapitated."

Phil felt his sanity rolling away.
"Completely decapitated."

THE KILLING GROUND

Jacob moved through the black woods like a shadow. Though he was a heavy, lumbering ox of a man, and his best years were far behind him, his stealth was admirable. He knew every tree trunk here, every thorn break, every stretch of shrubbery. He was dressed for the night, his clothing exclusively dark, his hat pulled down, a scarf wound over the lower part of his face. His boots were thick leather, their soles shod with iron, but they barely made a sound as he trod slowly forward. At his waist, a big hunting knife hung in its doeskin sheath; in his hands there was a shotgun, both its barrels cocked. His breath spilled before him in vaporous clouds, lingering in the ice-cold air, twisting wraith-like. It was the only movement. But Jacob wasn't taking chances. His keen countryman's eyes darted from side to side.

He knew the trap had sprung. He'd heard it even as he'd crouched in the hide a few dozen yards away. Now, it was somewhere just in front of him.

"You took my boy," he whispered, levelling the shotgun at chest-height. "You won't be taking this other little 'un."

With more caution than he'd ever shown in his life, he advanced into the next clearing. The brilliant winter moon illuminated it through naked, interlaced branches. A quick glance was all it took to establish that the first trap – the one he'd placed at the head of the trail leading towards the stables – was still open, which only left the second one. He turned and looked to the far side of the clearing. A patch of darkness concealed the second device. He'd placed it beneath the overhanging boughs of a holly tree, at the point where a narrow footpath snaked away towards the stream. Jacob hardly dared breathe. Scalp prickling, he raised the shotgun to his shoulder and proceeded like a soldier advancing on the enemy.

But still he could see nothing moving, and surely he ought to be able to by now?

Three yards remained; then two ...

Jacob felt distinctly uneasy.

Other shapes emerged from the blackness, pencil-thin shafts of moonlight spearing down through the conifers, glinting on the empty square of earth where the trap was supposed to be.

Jacob's unease turned to alarm.

His finger tightened on the trigger.

Where was it? *Where was the damn thing*?

He'd concealed it here with grasses and forest rubble, but it had gone. It had been moved. Yet how was that possible? That trap could have held an adult bear. And where was the chain? He'd dug down three feet so that he could anchor it under the root system. *How the hell had the bloody chain gone?*

He released the trigger, turning from side to side.

And only then did he sense the presence overhead.

He glanced up.

The ragged figure in the thick mass of holly regarded him silently. Though its veiled head was silhouetted in moonlight, its face, which was inclined down at him, was a blot of darkness.

Jacob backed away, fumbling with his shotgun, his gloves more a hindrance than a help.

He hadn't even smelled it. Surely to God he'd have smelled it?

He continued to retreat and continued to fumble, and one barrel fired, jettisoning its payload across the clearing.

Jacob cursed, uncocking the remaining barrel. He had to retreat further, had to get into a position from where he could aim. But now he only had one cartridge in the breech. Should he reload? He tore the scarf from his sweat-soaked face and glanced up again.

It had gone.

Simple as that.

One moment it had been high in the holly, a twisted thing, misshapen, grotesque, like the corpse of a felon thrown there after swinging on the gibbet.

And now it was gone.

He spun in a circle, shotgun to shoulder again, but now the moonlight dazzled him, sparkling from the sodden leaves and bracken.

"Damn you!" he said hoarsely. "Damn your desiccated hide!"

There was a *clash* of steel, like two heavy chopping-blades colliding.

Lightning struck Jacob's ankle: at first it was numbing, like a hammer-blow or axe-stroke, but very quickly the pain began. He looked down disbelievingly. The trap – the one he himself had set at the head of the trail to the stables – had clamped him. He knew immediately that his ankle had fractured; despite his sock and trouser leg, the steel teeth had sunk to the bone.

"Oh, Jesus," he gasped, as a loss of sensation shot up his leg. Had a nerve been severed? "Oh, Jesus Chriii …"

The limb buckled and he fell sideways, dropping his gun.

And in that instant, something came swiftly across the clearing towards him.

Jacob looked up with desperate eyes. It was black and shapeless, and it glided as it came. In the shafting moonlight, he caught vague glimpses of filthy, rotted garb. And now he could smell it too: the musk of a damp, empty room; the mildew of fungus-infested wrappings. When it stood directly in front of him, Jacob still couldn't see its face, and for that at least, he supposed, he ought to be thankful.

Slowly, almost tenderly, it placed something over his head.

"No," he breathed. "Please, no …"

He tried to jerk away, but there was a *twang* of snapping wire and another *clash* of steel, and this time the lightning struck Jacob in the neck: one blow to either side.

Again, the teeth bit deep.

Hot blood pumped out as he lost all motor-function and slumped, twitching, to the forest floor. From the throat down, he was a slab of ice. His vision faded fast.

His last coherent thought was that, after all these years of stalwart service, they'd probably write him off as a doddering old fool.

1

On a normal day, Ruth and Alec Whitchurch wouldn't have been allowed past the front door of Claridge's. But to be personally escorted up to its penthouse suite, then told to make themselves comfortable and be handed flutes of Dom Perignon 1998 was an experience neither of them had *ever* thought they'd have.

They sat in armchairs to either side of the huge art deco fireplace, sipping contentedly. This being the penthouse suite, they weren't actually in a bedroom, of which there were three, but were in the sitting room, and what a sitting room it was! Not only did it boast original eighteenth century furniture, it had marble fittings, polished parquet floors, and a barrel-vaulted ceiling from which hung a colossal chandelier. Its canary-yellow walls were decked with elegant oil paintings, but just in case the old-fashioned stuff didn't grab you, a cinema-sized plasma screen TV stood in one corner, above an all-in-one satellite receiver and hi-def DVD player. There was also a curtained slide-door, which opened onto the expansive rooftop terrace, though as it was now early December this was closed.

It was a bit of a surprise when the actual occupant of the suite came sauntering in, because he didn't really match up. Either to the opulence of his surroundings, or to his own name. Alec and Ruth recognised him nevertheless. Who wouldn't have? He was currently one of the most popular film stars on the planet, but he was shorter than they'd imagined and wearing horn-rimmed spectacles, which somehow reduced his air of authority. Despite this, they jumped to their feet.

"Don't stand on my account, folks," he said. "Here, have some more champagne." He nodded to the heavily-built security man who'd shown them up, indicating that he was to pour them another glass each. A magnum of the stuff stood nearby in a bucket of ice.

They nodded and smiled.

"Mike Duvalier," their host said. "As if you didn't know." Now that he wasn't putting on an accent, a strong California burr was noticeable in his all-American voice.

Half in and half out of an evening suit, he wore pressed pants and shiny black patent shoes. But his dress-shirt was open at the collar and cuffs, and he seemed to be having trouble with a bow tie, the strap of which had tangled into a knot.

"Can I perhaps help with that?" Ruth asked, showing her full set of nails.

"Uh? Oh, sure. If you don't mind." He handed it to her. "Had a pricy manicure early on, and my fingers are down to the quick. There's supposed to be a butler with this suite, but I don't like guys I don't know hanging around." Duvalier caught sight of himself in the beaten bronze facing over the fireplace, and groaned. "Goddamn, look at this."

His hair, which was short and very black – possibly dyed black, Alec thought, now that he was seeing it in real life – was mussed and unruly. The movie star ran an analytical finger down the side of his jaw, presumably to check his most recent shave, which no doubt had cost him a small fortune. He didn't seem pleased with the result.

"Here," Ruth said. She'd unknotted the offending tie and handed it back.

Duvalier took it from her, and gave her a smile of gratitude that was almost boyish.

Alec wondered how it was possible that this man had convincingly led an elite corps of space marines to capture a moon base overrun by gelatinous, flesh-eating aliens; or had evaded the finest Sioux warriors, as they'd relentlessly hunted him through the wilds of nineteenth century Montana after massacring his wagon train; or had broken the biggest organised crime network on the eastern seaboard, despite being the hardest drinking cop in the NYPD.

"I guess I'm not quite what you expected?" Duvalier said.

Alec blinked. He hadn't meant to be caught staring.

"I'll be frank," Duvalier added. "You guys aren't what I was expecting either. When they told me the best private investigators in London were a husband and wife team, I thought they were jerking me around. But even after I'd gotten used to the idea, the last thing I imagined was Ken and Barbie."

They gave no immediate reaction to this.

"What I mean is, you're both a lot younger than I thought."

Ruth smiled sweetly. With her soft, blonde hair and slim, athletic figure – which currently looked both smart *and* sexy in her shell-grey Jaeger suit (shoes by Jimmy Choo) – she seemed much less than her thirty-five years. On the other hand, it wasn't often that Alec, who was forty and felt it, had his own age questioned. However, he liked to work out, and was tanned and trim, and as Ruth had recently been making an effort to bring his wardrobe into the twenty-first century, and now had him in his best Savile Row casuals, he supposed he was a visual improvement on the heavyweight, saggy-faced Scotland Yard growler the film star had probably been anticipating.

"You guys look more like actors than I do," Duvalier said. "You really ex-cops?"

Alec nodded. "For seven years I was operational DCI at the Major Incident Command. That's the Metropolitan Police's serious crime unit."

"DCI?"

"Detective Chief Inspector, an equivalent role to your precinct captain. Ruth was one of my sergeants."

"So why did you leave?" Duvalier put in his cuff links. "Pardon me for being blunt, but I need to know."

"We got married," Ruth replied.

"So?"

"We wanted to have a family."

"And?"

"Neither of us believes that cops make good parents."

"What, and private investigators do?"

"We only became private investigators after," she said coolly.

"After what?"

"After we found we *couldn't* have a family."

"Ah, I see."

"There was some politics in there too," Alec added. "These days, there are elements in the British police service – academic types, people who've been fast-tracked in from university – who think it's about doing what's fashionable rather than what's right."

"Criminals aren't criminals anymore," Ruth explained, "they're 'disadvantaged persons'."

"Habitual offenders are no longer evil little swine," Alec added. "Now they're 'maladjusted'."

"I get you," Duvalier said, fastening his tie which, considering the problems he'd had unfastening it, he did with a flourish. "That's one viewpoint we share, which is a good sign. Not that I need one. My lawyer's got plenty connections over here, and you fellas come highly recommended."

Alec thanked him. "We have our areas of expertise. What exactly is the job?"

"It's quite unusual." Duvalier dragged a brush through his hair. "Not the sort of thing I would normally hire a PI to look into. That's why I'll need you to sign an affidavit that you'll keep this whole thing to yourselves. But first – I'm running a little late. Can you guys take a ride with me to Greenwich?" He pronounced it 'Green Witch'. "Believe it or not, I've agreed to attend at charity dinner at the Royal Naval College there. In the new movie, I'm a captain in Nelson's fleet – lots of seafaring action. Got to master my English accent first, of course. That's why I'm over here for the next couple of months."

Alec and Ruth exchanged discomforted glances. With their office/flat in Bayswater, it wouldn't be ideal for them to get stranded in Greenwich on a bustling Friday evening.

"Don't worry," Duvalier said. "You can ride there with me. I'll have my driver bring you back again after. It's just so we can talk. As I said before, the job's pretty unusual."

2

"I need to be absolutely certain you won't tell anyone about this. I mean, obviously you've not signed on yet, so I can't legally oblige you. But perhaps you can give me your word? When even the tiniest bit of gossip slips out about someone like me, you'd be amazed how the story grows with the telling."

Ruth and Alec were sitting alongside Duvalier in the back of a smoke-grey Bentley as it cruised through the centre of London. By the size and weight of the vehicle, it was armour-plated. In the front there were two suited American security men, one driving, the other – the broad-shouldered, thick-necked one who had shown them up to the star's penthouse suite – in the passenger seat.

"No problem," Alec replied.

Duvalier nodded. "Okay, here it is. I don't know if you heard, but about nine months ago I purchased a house over here in the UK. A country house, a place called Killingly Hall."

Ruth mused. "Sounds familiar."

"It's pretty pleasant, even if I say so myself," Duvalier said. "It's in Herefordshire, on the border country with Wales. It was once a baronial seat. Don't know if that's impressive these days or not."

"Fairly impressive," Alec said, thinking of their own apartment, which had cost half a million yet still had only two bedrooms and a kitchen so small you couldn't swing a cat in it.

"Anyway," Duvalier added, "me and Rosa had been looking for an English home for quite some time. I make a lot of movies over here, as you probably know. Rosa doesn't, but for the moment she's not working as much as usual."

Rosanna Duvalier – or Rosanna Perdita, to use her professional moniker – had previously been a beautiful but little-known actress-singer from Mexico, whose commercial viability had skyrocketed after her glitzy Hollywood wedding to Duvalier. Despite this, there was nothing to suggest that career prospects had been foremost in her mind when she'd said "I do". They'd now been married eight years, and were deemed to have a strong, happy relationship.

"Rosa's got projects lined up, but she's also looking after our daughter," Duvalier said. "Wants to be a 'proper mom', at least as much as she's able. Anyway, we thought it would be cool, since I'm over here until spring anyway, to have a traditional English Christmas. A Dickens-type thing, you know. All our best friends up at Killingly for the whole of the holidays."

"Sounds lovely," Ruth said.

"We thought that too." Duvalier had removed his glasses before leaving the hotel, and was now wearing contacts, which briefly gave a glazed appearance to his sharp blue eyes. "But about three months ago, Rosa was over here with me. We were checking the place out – Killingly, I mean – when she heard something that freaked her a little."

He paused for several long moments.

"And this was?" Alec finally asked.

The actor seemed unsure how to continue.

"We may *look* like Ken and Barbie, Mr. Duvalier," Ruth said. "But nothing you can say will shock us, I assure you."

Duvalier bit his lip. "Well … try this for size. Rosa's a Catholic. I mean, she's like a *serious* Catholic. I had to convert just to get her to marry me."

Ruth remembered hearing about this; she'd thought it odd considering the last movie Rosanna Perdita had appeared in was an LA-set gangster flick, in which she'd played a barrio whore and had stripped off twice to perform hot sex scenes. One of the genuinely unpleasant things about being a movie star, she supposed: whether you liked it or not, your life was divided into two very different halves, the reality and the fantasy.

Duvalier was still talking. "As well as being a devout Catholic, which gives her a kind of spiritual side already,

I suppose, Rosa comes from a rural background. And rural Mexico even now is … well, it's a pretty superstitious place."

He left that hanging, so Alec had to encourage him. "Go on."

"In a nutshell, we bought the house without knowing about its background. It's very old, obviously. That didn't bother us. That was part of its appeal. But then we found out it had one hell of a ghost story attached to it."

Neither Alec nor Ruth registered surprise, but waited patiently for the next revelation. Duvalier eyed them curiously, wondering if they'd already taken him for a flake.

"Mr. Duvalier," Ruth finally said, "ghost stories in English country houses are ten-a-penny."

He shook his head adamantly. "Not like this one. This ghost, or monster, or whatever it is … this *ghoul*, is … well, it's supposed to eat children."

There was silence as the car negotiated the log-jammed traffic on Tower Bridge. Great as Duvalier's acting skills were, at that moment he had tremendous difficulty concealing his embarrassment. He couldn't cover the deep flush in his cheek.

"That's all I know about it," he added. "I haven't had time to look into the story myself, I'm way too busy. But apparently it's pretty difficult to get local people to staff the place if it involves having to live in. There are supposedly genuine stories that something horrible haunts the hall, and that it snatches kids and eats them."

"Who told you this?" Alec asked quietly.

"An old guy we got talking to in the local pub."

"I see." Despite his best efforts, Alec's mirthful contempt for bar-side rumourists was implicit in his expression.

"Our gamekeeper told us a similar story," Duvalier added hurriedly.

Alec still shook his head. "No disrespect, Mr. Duvalier, but these guys are likely to be full of shit. I mean *full* of it. A big name movie star arrives, and immediately they want to be more to him than bumpkin peasants. As scary stories go, it's not even very original."

"My thoughts too, but it's not me you've got to convince."

"It's Rosa," Ruth said.

He nodded. "Our daughter, Claudette, is six years old, and she's absolutely the apple of her mom's eye. All our attempts to have children were failures until Rosa got herself some extensive fertility treatment. Since then, to compensate, she's kind of over-protective. As I say, she's also got this superstitious streak, and those two don't make a good combination, trust me. I mean picture this: Claudette's birth is difficult; she's small and needs a lot of hospital time. Finally, though, she comes home. Then she suffers a couple of childhood illnesses, which worry us a lot. Eventually that's over too. Everyone relaxes again, and then something like this happens."

"But *nothing's* happened yet," Alec said.

Duvalier gestured hopefully. "With luck it never will, but that's where you guys come in. Go through the records, talk to everyone you can. Just prove to me, so that I can prove to Rosa, that it's all a bunch of crap."

"Mr. Duvalier," Ruth said. "It'll be a bare-faced lie, a bit of mischief cooked up in a pub tap-room."

"If it is, fine. Believe me, that'd be music to my ears."

"You really want to pay us our normal rate just so we can come up with a solution like that?" Alec wondered.

As a rule, when he and Ruth worked a case together they charged £25,000 up front, and from the end of the first month £1000 a day. Possibly Duvalier didn't realise this.

"Money's no object," he said.

"In which case, why don't you just sell the place?" Ruth asked. "I mean, sorry for saying this, but your wife clearly gets uptight. Would anything we say *ever* make Killingly Hall good for her? Won't she always be worried about going there, at least for as long as Claudette's a child? Sell it, buy somewhere else. That'll solve the problem."

"And then a similar problem will crop up at the next place," Duvalier said, "and at the place after that. I *like* Killingly Hall." His voice became impassioned. "I've owned it less than a year and already I'm in love with it. And I'm determined to have this Dickensian Christmas. The invitations have gone out, the plans are made."

"And Rosa's prepared to come over and attend?" Alec asked.

"She and Claudette fly in next week. It was a fight, but I got her to agree as long as some expert – someone like you guys – was able to categorically assure us that this *being*, this child-eater, is fictional."

The investigators exchanged bewildered glances. Ruth finally said: "We're just detectives. Wouldn't you be better employing a medium or clairvoyant?"

"Oh Jesus, none of that! That'd just make things worse. It'd reinforce Rosa's belief in this baloney. Besides, like I said, I'm not sure we're actually dealing with a traditional ghost here."

"No," Alec said pointedly. "We're dealing with something that eats children."

Duvalier glanced round at him. "You find that ridiculous, uh?"

Alec did, but probably no more so than the notion that this well-dressed but short, rather worried-looking man could convince the world he was a dashing skipper in Nelson's heroic navy. Of course, Duvalier would soon be on the silver screen doing just that. So it wasn't an encouraging comparison, all things considered.

3

If the British Library, which boasted that it held over 150 million books and documents, some allegedly dating back to as early as 300 BC, couldn't shed light on the case, then Alec didn't know which institution would.

However, he made some ground that morning before he even set out from home. A search for Killingly Hall on a 'historic houses' website produced the following chunk of information:

Killingly Hall
Tyberton, Herefordshire

Despite its modern appearance (the current building dates from the early 20th century), Killingly has a history that spans over 900 years. Originally constructed in the late 11th century to hold a troublesome corner of the Welsh march, it eventually passed from royal control into the ownership of the De Souza family, Norman warlords who replaced its timber ramparts with stone, and held it successfully until 1138, when it was captured by King Stephen and granted to his loyal subject Gilbert de Villehardoin, Earl of Worcester. Extensive rebuilding work was completed in 1285 when, on the orders of Edward I, a new keep, a barbican and a stronger curtain *wall were added as protection against the Welsh. Untouched by the Wars of the Roses, it went into a slow decline during the later Middle Ages, passing from one owner to another, none of whom were comfortable in its cold, military environment. In 1586 the historian William Cornell called it: "A sad remnant of earlier days. A melancholy ruin, all but uninhabitable." What remained of the medieval building was destroyed completely by Cromwellian troops during the Civil War, and reconstruction only commenced in 1683, when a friend of Charles II, Percival Hart, sought to make it his family home. He and his descendants occupied the new-built hall, now a traditional country house rather than a castle, for several generations, continually embellishing it until it was described by an 18th century antiquarian as: "A most delectable edifice, founded on a handsome base of Wren-age design". Unfortunately, we can only take the antiquarian's word for this, as the hall was gutted by fire in 1798, and had to be completely demolished two years later. It was rebuilt, but a further disastrous fire damaged it in 1837 and it was subsequently abandoned. It remained empty and decaying for three quarters of a century, until purchased by the industrialist George Jolley who, like Percival Hart, was seeking an ancestral home. The present building, a compact, grey stone structure dressed up in the castle style with crenellations and tall, narrow windows, was finished in 1914, and then filled with rare paintings and antique furniture. For a brief time after Jolley's death in 1936, it became a country club but, in the second half of the 20th century more discerning owners restored it to its stately home grandeur, a condition in which it still, happily, stands today.*

It was interesting stuff, but pretty dry. What was more, as Killingly Hall didn't seem to have played a *major* role in historical events, Alec felt he'd be lucky to find anything else. He was wrong, however. Once he got to the library, the information he'd already gleaned proved useful. It led him quickly to additional research material which, when it was all put together, painted a grim but informative picture.

An assistant brought him a textbook charting the history of Herefordshire. Its front cover bore a photograph of what looked like an agonised human head carved at the end of a church pew. After checking in the index, Alec found an immediate reference to the De Souza family, which, when he flicked back to it, took him to a chapter concerned with the so-called 'English Anarchy', an internal war that tore the kingdom apart between 1135 and 1154.

Knowing nothing about this period, he began to read.

Commencing as a dynastic struggle between King Stephen, the grandson of William the Conqueror, and his cousin, Matilda Plantagenet, it seemed the English Anarchy soon turned into a miniature holocaust. It commenced in straightforward fashion, with the main players seizing key castles and mobilising large armies. Soon, however, these organised powers had annihilated each other on the battlefield, as a result of which all law and order broke down. The realm fragmented as mercenaries and bands of deserters went on a non-stop rampage. There was robbery and rape on a massive scale. Even those barons not involved in the conflict saw the opportunity to sack towns and wage private feuds with each other. Bridges were burned, crops were trampled and destroyed. Famine followed, and then pestilence. "For nineteen long winters Christ and his angels slept," one chronicler wrote. “Every man stole from another if he could.” Numberless lives were lost, and entire family-lines ceased to exist, including many among the nobility. According to the book, the De Souza clan was no exception.

Alec read on, not sure it was relevant but fascinated to know more.

From the onset of the Anarchy, Bertram de Souza, Lord of Tyberton, had declared for Matilda. But the tide turned quickly against him. In 1139, while he was away fighting on the would-be queen’s behalf, King Stephen sent a force under the Earl of Worcester to besiege the De Souza castle, later to be called Killingly but at this early stage known by the name the Welsh had given it: Brac Cannor.

Bertram’s wife, Morgana, had only a hundred knights and men-at-arms at her disposal, but she refused to surrender. Several times the royal army tried to take the castle, but it was always repulsed. At length, King Stephen himself took charge of the siege. He ordered the construction of a hundred gibbets in the meadow beyond the castle’s west wall, then sent a message to Lady Morgana that everyone inside, herself and her young son Piers included, would be hanged when eventually captured – unless they surrendered peacefully, in which case all would be spared. He added, as a footnote, that Morgana’s husband, Bertram, was now dead, having been slain in battle.

Fearing the worst and with supplies running low, Lady Morgana accepted the king’s offer. The garrison departed the castle, only to be seized by the king’s men who, with joyous deceit, set each one of them dangling. The only lives saved were those of Lady Morgana and her child. These two were placed by King Stephen in the charge of

Gilbert de Villehardoin, the aforesaid Earl of Worcester, who was granted Brac Cannor in reward for his efforts.

Seeing them as a threat to his new inheritance, Villehardoin might have done away with the two hostages immediately, but the story about Bertram de Souza's death had been a ruse. Morgana's husband was still alive and fighting in Matilda's name. So instead of killing his captives, Villehardoin imprisoned them in their own castle, in an oubliette, the deepest, dankest dungeon he could find. There, they were kept in complete darkness and fed and watered only sparingly. In 1141, when Villehardoin learned that Bertram de Souza had died at the battle of Winchester, the food and water ceased altogether and the oubliette was sealed, condemning the unfortunate pair to death by starvation. Villehardoin continued to reside at Brac Cannor for another two years, until the loss of his own young son, at which point he returned to his former residence of Worcester.

The chapter then moved to other matters, and Alec laid the book aside. Killingly had a blood-stained history – there was no doubt of that, but it didn't provide many clues for the investigation. A short time later, however, he was given a second tome, this a lot thicker and much older. It was bound in musty, yellowed linen and titled *Traditions of the Cotswold Country*, it promised to be 'a treatise on the myths and folklore of the western lands'.

Alec leafed through it. To call this book prose-heavy would have been an understatement. It was written in a weighty, unimaginative style, and said nothing in one sentence if three paragraphs would do instead. But the assistant had marked a page for him, and as soon as Alec saw it his interest was aroused.

It was headed:

Of the depredations of Baroness Morgana

The first section reiterated what he already knew concerning the terrible fate of Morgana de Souza and her son. But then it went further, adding material which, though it owed more to legend than historical fact, was gruesome and disturbing:

The callous band who took possession of Brac Cannor were to pay dearly, as were others who would follow them. For their brutal actions unleashed a hideous curse.

As she and her child lay dying in their underground prison, Baroness Morgana took it on herself to make a pact with Satan. She sought to ensure that, for all time, none but she would hold sway in this ancient family home. In return, the Dark Lord exacted a ghastly price. The Baroness, he demanded, must prove her fealty by devouring her own child. As the young Piers had already expired, it was not perhaps as horrible a prospect as it might sound, but even so, the woman – now a thing demented, a living-horror of the darkness – fell upon her cannibal feast with unnatural gusto.

Soon afterwards, it was said, peasant children living on the manor estates of Brac Cannor began to disappear, and searches located only their bones. Strangers were questioned and the district combed, but no answers were forthcoming. Earl Villehardoin became fearful. Stories reached his ears that a monster was walking at night: something twisted and malformed; something that hungered for the flesh of little ones; yet something which, according to those who had glimpsed it, had the dimensions of a female. When his own young son was taken in this fashion, Earl Villehardoin lost his mind. He took to wearing horsehair shirts and to flogging himself, and a month later he and his household abandoned Brac Cannor altogether. But the nightmare persisted. At night, folk whispered, the bloodthirsty revenant of Baroness Morgana would prowl the castle and adjoining precincts, preying like some voracious she-wolf on any child she found.

For centuries this grisly shadow hung over Brac Cannor, even after the castle had been demolished and another house built there instead. No proof, of course, has ever been offered, and many now scoff. Yet in the spring of 1683, when deep excavations were made among the foundations of the original stone fortress, an airless crypt was uncovered, a tiny aperture that had once been bricked up. It contained a single, small skeleton, the bones of which were scarred as though by teeth. When attempts were made to bring the skeleton to the surface, it crumbled to dust. The workmen who'd found it refused to re-enter the place, but insisted there'd been no trace of a second skeleton there.

Later, the foundations were broken to rubble and ploughed beneath the ground, so that nothing at all remained of that Hadean pit.

Alec wasn't sure all this was worth a morning's work, but it wasn't immaterial to the case. He scanned the pages of interest and emailed them to Ruth, who was at home making phone-calls. With luck, she'd gained more ground than he had.

The 'System', as they called it, was an unofficial network of private eyes, informants and – some might say 'crooked' though others would argue 'sympathetic' – police officers. Ruth was currently tapping into it. The kind of intel it provided didn't come cheap, but as well as agreeing to play the Whitchurches their full fee, Mike Duvalier had given them a generous expense account, so on this occasion it would pose no problem.

Ruth returned Alec's call shortly before lunchtime, as he emerged onto Euston Road and stood in the gothic shadow of St. Pancras railway station. "Hi," he said. "Anything?"

"Yeah, bits and pieces. First off, that document you sent me – the one about Baroness Morgana and her depredations. That's quite interesting. Are you buying into it?"

"I wouldn't say I'm buying into it exactly. It's hokum, isn't it. Course, it might help a bit. It explains where those local yokels got their ideas from."

"Will it do the job, though? Will it convince Mrs. Duvalier that everything's a-okay, or will it have exactly the opposite effect?"

Alec hailed a passing cab and climbed in. "Bayswater Road, mate. Cheers." He continued on the phone. "Well, if she believes in fairy stories like this, she's got problems *we* can't resolve for her."

For some reason, Ruth sounded less certain. "It might be more than a fairy story."

"What are you talking about?"

"I've been on the System all morning, and results are starting to come back. Get this: Killingly Hall is in the West Mercia Police force area, right?"

"Yeah."

"Well, their computer files go back to the mid-1970s, so that's as far as we're able to go at present. But from that period – 1976 to be precise – in their westernmost divisions there are fourteen cases of missing children outstanding."

Alec was startled. "Fourteen!"

"The ages range from eleven to three. Two of them, the oldest two, were regarded as runaways. Apparently, there were problems in their family backgrounds."

"That still leaves twelve."

"Correct. And of the remaining twelve, seven cases are still active."

"Why not all of them?"

"First of all the time factor. Who's got the resources to investigate back past twenty years? But there do seem to be other possibilities. In one case a close relative was the prime suspect. It was never proved, but he's now dead anyway. In two others there was a suggestion of accidental death. On both those occasions the missing child was last seen on the banks of a river: the first on the Wye, the second on the Dore."

"When does the most recent one date to?" he asked.

"Three years ago. Doesn't sound as though they're making much ground. Even that enquiry's getting scaled down now."

"I don't believe it. Twelve missing kids in one area."

"It's a fairly wide area, remember. It's rural, and it covers a number of sub-divisions."

"Are any cases deemed to be connected?"

"They were at first. They got highlighted by Operation Enigma[1] in the late '90s. But nothing came from it. There's just no evidence."

"I can't believe there isn't a major panic on."

"There probably would be, but you know what it's like."

And that was true. Alec *did* know what it was like. When he'd been a kid himself, any missing youngster

---

[1] A major Scotland Yard operation intended to review unsolved murders throughout England and Wales, in particular where modern techniques had suggested that a serial predator might be at large.

was an event, especially in the wake of the Moors Murders. These days things were so much different. Most police station porches were papered with the faces of children, teenagers, vulnerable persons of every sort who'd simply dropped out of sight. There were dedicated 'missing-persons' units up and down the country, but they only made a dent in the floodtide of absences.

"You checked any force areas outside West Mercia?" he asked.

"Dyfed Powys is next door," she said, "just over the border. I'm still waiting on the results for that."

"Are there any disappearances specific to Killingly Hall itself?"

"Not really. But ..." Ruth paused. "It'd be interesting to see how far its medieval manorial boundaries extended, don't you think?"

"Yes," Alec said, unable to believe that he was actually contemplating such a notion. "Yes, I do."

4

As they drove west, the weather turned more seasonal. The autumnal wind and rain of mid-December gave way to a crisp winter chill. In the West Country it had actually been snowing: a thin covering lay over the low hills and gentle valleys. The leafless hedgerows were thickly frosted, a cool, powder blue sky arching overhead. Thankfully the roads, even the secondary roads in this primarily rural region, had been gritted.

"You know," Ruth said, as they tore along in Alec's MG, "just say for the sake of argument that there *is* a serial killer or serial kidnapper in Herefordshire. The chances are that, of these nineteen kids" – it had now become nineteen, because five new names had been added to the list courtesy of her enquiries with Dyfed-Powys – "at least half will still have disappeared in non-suspicious circumstances. The two that were thought to be runaways probably *were* runaways. The chances are that others were runaways too. The final tally will be far less terrifying than it actually looks."

Alec shrugged. "Are you making this speech to me or rehearsing it for Mike Duvalier?"

"He's not going to like it, is he?"

"It isn't all bad."

Alec was right in that respect. Before they'd compiled their final report, checks with contacts at Scotland Yard and the National Crime Group had revealed no current investigations related to any form of 'child-snatching' in the district they were now entering. Not only that: notes filed by detectives involved in Operation Enigma had addressed the high number of missing youngsters there in recent decades, but had referred to 'unfortunate sets of coincidences', citing the various social problems blighting the area's larger towns – drug addiction, abusive parents, child delinquency and the like – and the fact that people were frequently lost in the rivers Dore and Wye, two large waterways which, because they both ran swiftly to the sea, rarely gave up their dead. To complete the picture, Alec and Ruth had used the System to make random enquiries with police force areas in other parts of the country, and had uncovered similar numbers of mispers[2], so it wasn't a phenomenon unique to the Killingly Hall region.

[2] Police parlance for missing vulnerable persons.

Despite this, and the fact they'd been on the case for two weeks, something still nagged at Ruth. "I can't help feeling that we've not really done our job."

"Why?" Alec asked. "All Duvalier's paying for is intel. That's what we're providing him with."

"Why do we need to deliver it personally?"

"I guess so he can question us. Maybe so his wife can too. Plus it's not as if we can email him this sort of stuff, is it?"

The documentation they'd amassed, now sealed in two bulging buff folders, sat on the back seat. The first and larger of the two was all police-related and contained photocopies of crime reports, witness statements, misper dossiers and the like, going back decades. Needless to say, it was all classified and their possession of it was highly illegal. The second folder was less packed but more legitimate: it comprised articles relating to the medieval legends of the district; not just copies from books and print-outs from the Net, but maps, newspaper cuttings, and verbal accounts taken from local folk courtesy of the System. It did not, however, add a great deal to the data Alec had collected on the first day.

They drove on, enjoying the clear sky and snowy countryside. On the radio, Luther Vandross was singing *Have Yourself A Merry Little Christmas*. They stopped for lunch at a thatch-roofed pub, the interior of which was hung with evergreens and fairy lights, then a few miles down the road called at a garage for petrol. While Alec was refilling the tank, Ruth browsed in the shop and picked up a slim softback volume titled *Mysterious Place Names of the West Country*. As they hit the road again, she read aloud one particular section.

"'Killingly: the private demesnes of Killingly Hall, formerly a baronial seat in the west hundreds of

Herefordshire, close to the Welsh border. Once a wild, remote region, this is now a picturesque landscape of orchards, hop-yards and rolling green hills, studded here and there with atmospheric *olde worlde* villages. Not without justification is it called 'the Garden of the West'. However, the unusual place name 'Killingly' is believed to derive from gruesome events in the past, as seen in the conjunction of two words: the Anglo-Danish 'killing', a participle of the verb we still use today, 'to kill', and the Middle English noun 'ley' or 'lea', which means 'woodland'. The assumption, therefore, is that 'Killingly' stems from the phrase 'killing wood' or perhaps 'killing ground', as in a place where executions or possibly murders occurred'."

"Probably refers to that mass hanging in the twelfth century," Alec said. "The one mentioned in the history book."

"Could be, though whoever wrote this last paragraph might disagree: 'The original Norman castle that once occupied the site was called 'Brac Cannor'. The name 'Killingly' only seems to have entered common use around the mid seventeenth century, by which time the long-derelict estate had acquired a grim reputation'."

"Well there's nothing grim about the way it's looking," Alec commented.

The further west they headed the wilder yet more scenic the vista. The neatly hedged fields gave way to sweeps of rugged, upland pasture where dry-stone walling became the boundary builder's choice. The Cotswold market towns, all uniformly built from the same honey-coloured limestone, vanished, to be replaced by timber-framed black and white farmsteads tucked into the folds of the ever more undulant hills. Trees were less abundant, so the sky seemed to broaden; as day turned to dusk, purple snow-clouds had appeared, yet far to the west it was clear and glacially cold, scattered stars like pips of ice shimmering down on the snow-capped Welsh mountains, turning their distant peaks a luminous white. It was against this backdrop that they finally arrived at the gates of the Killingly Hall estate.

They were greeted by a bunch of journalists and photographers in scarves and overcoats, standing around cars and vans, beating their gloved hands, blowing clouds of vapour. As the tall gates swung open to admit Alec and Ruth, the frustrated news pack could only watch, though one or two ventured forth and snapped shots through the MG's windows. On the other side of the gate two security men emerged from a small gatehouse. They wore black overcoats, black scarves, and black woolly gloves. The first one was hugely broad with a neck like a tree trunk. Ruth and Alec recognised him from Claridge's. Alec wound down his window.

"Howdy, folks," the security guy said without smiling. Now, as they looked him over properly, they saw that he was handsome and tanned, but had a single nasty scar down his cheek. His flat-topped crewcut gave him a military air. He extended a hand. "Lane Karswell. We met in London."

"Hey," Alec said.

"The boss is up at the hall. He's expecting you. Sorry, but I've got to check in your trunk first. We're under orders not to take any chances."

"No problem." Alec popped the boot.

A few moments later they moved on, following a cindery drive, which ran alongside a frozen brook, before winding away through numerous stands of trees, mainly beech, their tall trunks forming black stanchions against the carpet of snow. Finally they emerged in manicured parkland where the main house stood. Full darkness had fallen, so the house was lit brilliantly, making it an impressive sight. Though its architecture owed everything to the early twentieth century, it retained the aura of a bastion on the edge of wilderness. It was a solid, square mansion, built entirely from granite. It had been castellated in the mock-medieval style and large areas of the walls were clad with luxuriant ivy, but aside from that it lacked elaborate decoration. It was huge; they guessed it must have had space for thirty or more bedrooms. The windows that ran along its east-facing frontage were tall and narrow, paned with mullioned glass and rosy with firelight.

"Just how I imagined Baskerville Hall to look," Ruth said as they drove up.

"We're a long way from Dartmoor," Alec replied.

"Yeah. But how far are we from a hound?"

5

The interior of the hall was at least as regal as the exterior, though again it retained that robust aura of border stronghold.

The grand front door opened straight into the main drawing room, a vast chamber with stone-flagged floors and a high, cross-timbered ceiling. All the usual accoutrements were present: suits of armour in the corners, old masters on the oak-panelled walls, alongside antlered skulls, antique weaponry and heraldic banners.

Mike Duvalier, clad in a tracksuit and sneakers, and wearing his glasses, was seated on a leather sofa in front of a magnificent stone hearth in which a winter fire blazed. He was sipping what looked like a vitamin drink, and at the same time working his way through a great pile of DVDs. On closer inspection they were brand new copies of his latest movie, in which he played a Bond-type secret agent on the run from his own side after being framed; he had a black marker pen, and was carefully adding his signature to each disc.

"Welcome," he said, without looking up. "Sorry about this, I won't keep you long. These are Christmas presents for my guests. Suppose it looks kind of conceited, but let's live in the real world. With my autograph on it, any one of these could fetch a couple of thousand dollars on Ebay. Drinks?"

The replied in the negative, so the security man who'd admitted them to the hall and had been hovering around in the background withdrew. Another second passed, before Duvalier told them to take a seat and asked what they'd got for him. Ruth sat in the nearest armchair, but Alec remained standing as he handed over the two folders. Duvalier unsealed them and began to pick through their contents.

For several moments Alec outlined their findings, before the actor, rather abruptly, interrupted him. "So what's your gut feeling?"

"Sorry?" Alec said.

"You guys are the lead-investigators in this case. What's your gut feeling?"

"Well, there's only actually been one proven child murder in this area in modern times: in 1964, a rape-strangulation. A local farm worker got life for it."

Duvalier didn't seem convinced. His expression was suddenly grim, even agitated. "And all these unexplained disappearances?"

"We can only give you the facts, Mr. Duvalier," Ruth said. "Some of them are missing-presumed-dead, others are just missing. None of them have generated full-blown murder enquiries."

Duvalier took out one particular document, unfolded it, and found that it was a large map. "What's this exactly?"

"It's the Killingly Hall manor estate," Alec replied, "late seventeenth century."

Duvalier shoved the DVDs aside and spread the map on the coffee table. He gazed down at it, though for a moment was so troubled that it didn't seem to make much sense to him. In truth, it would have made little sense to anyone who didn't specifically know what they were looking for. It was an exact reproduction of an original, so any writing on it, either down the edges or on the map itself, was minute in size and archaic in script. The map wasn't in colour and there were few recognisable features on it to a modern eye, aside from a couple of river tributaries and a quilt-work zone that might have signified arable land. More distinct was the red biro with which someone had recently encircled a large central area and marked out a few small crosses and dates.

Duvalier shook his head. "And this is relevant because … ?"

"It's more for reference than anything else," Alec said. "Everything inside the red line was the property of the lord of the manor. Everyone who lived there was his tenant. It's a pretty wide area, as you can see, eight or nine square miles, much wider than the estate is now. But there was probably a lot more than this in the eleventh century when the manor was first created. Unfortunately there are no maps dating from then. This is the earliest one we could find, and we searched exhaustively."

"But what am I supposed to read into it?" Duvalier asked.

This time Ruth answered. "Morgana de Souza, who was the lady of the manor in the 1130s, is clearly the origin of this cannibal legend that's frightened your wife. According to tradition, the deal she made with the Devil was only applicable to the manor estate because that was the geographic area she wanted to deny to her enemies."

"Ah. So you picked this up to see if any of the kids who've gone missing in our time might correspond with that?"

"That's what the red crosses indicate," she said. "This map's totally different from a modern map, of course. Apart from these blocks of farmland, most of it is untamed wildwood. It would have been even more untamed back in the Middle Ages. These days there's a whole network of roads, towns and villages that aren't on here, but the land itself hasn't changed. These red crosses indicate roughly the places where the recent kids went missing."

Duvalier pursed his lips. "Six in total: '78, '81, '85, '92, '99, 2002."

He paused to ponder, and they knew exactly what he was thinking. 1978 to 2002: twenty-four years. A long time, but not too long to be the timespan of a killer's career. Finally he focused on something else, a cross in the lower left corner of the estate, this one marked in green biro.

"What does this indicate?"

"That's the murder in 1964," Alec said.

"So that one was inside the manor boundary as well?"

"Yes, but the guy who did it confessed, and never retracted his story before he died in jail in 1983. You don't need to worry about that one."

Duvalier gave him a look. "*You* clearly worried about it. Otherwise you wouldn't have put it there."

For a second Alec couldn't answer that. Now that he considered it, he wondered why he'd included the green cross.

"We just wanted to give you the facts, Mr. Duvalier," Ruth put in. "All of them."

The actor stood up. "And you've certainly done that. You're thorough, you guys, there's no denying." He glanced again at the map; then dropped it on the table. "How do you fancy staying on here for the next couple of weeks?"

"Excuse me?" Ruth said.

"I'll double your rate."

She glanced at Alec, who seemed equally surprised, but who shrugged and said: "We've done everything we can. We'd just be killing time."

Ruth would have added that there was further reference material they could check – she currently had six different researchers looking for lost literature concerning Killingly Hall – but in truth she wasn't expecting anything from them.

However, Duvalier seemed keen on the idea. "Rather than having you continue to investigate, I was thinking more of attaching you to the security team. Just for the duration of the holiday."

Again they looked at each other, unsure.

"I don't understand what else we can contribute," Alec said.

"Hell, you know about this stuff. You've researched it, you're focused on it. You'd be good to have around if something happens."

"Mr. Duvalier, the chance of something happening is so slim there's honestly no point considering it."

The actor chuckled. "Fellas, you know the state of play here. I don't believe in this supernatural abductor any more than you. But Rosa does … and she especially will when she sees all this. I can't hide it from her. It was for her peace of mind that I commissioned it in the first place. And what the hell, if you end up having nothing to do while you're here, all the better. Enjoy the festivities and get paid for it. Unless there's somewhere else you need to be? You've already told me you don't have any kids."

Ruth and Alec considered the alternative Christmases facing them.

First of all, they could go to Ruth's grandma's, a cramped terraced house in Huddersfield, where they'd share the season with a clutch of screaming nephews and nieces, everywhere treading on streamers, mince pie crumbs and broken ornaments, being constantly plied with booze even though they were muzzy-headed from the night before, endlessly having to listen to Slade and Wizzard played at mega-volume, and then of course sitting in silence for the Queen's Speech on Christmas Day afternoon. Secondly, they could go and stay with Alec's mum and dad in their seaside bungalow in West Sussex, where the atmosphere would be chilly regardless of whether it was snowing down there, as Alec's silver-rinsed, upper-middle class mother strongly disapproved of his having married 'below himself'. The turkey would be good and there'd be generous tots of sherry, but the laughs would be few and far between, despite (or possibly because of) the hats and crackers, and they'd still have to watch the Queen's Speech on Christmas Day. Thirdly, they could spend it at home together, enjoying each other's company, because who else did you need aside from the love of your life?, but maybe thinking it a little quiet, and – particularly during the Queen's Speech

– missing the excited squeals of children as they unwrapped oodles of presents.

Or they could spend it here.

"Tomorrow night we're having a traditional Christmas Eve," Duvalier added, "with everyone in Dickensian costume. We've got musicians, mummers. There'll be dances, games. We've got one hell of a spread too."

"And you said you'd … *double* our fee?" Alec asked tentatively.

"Sure. No problem."

"Mr. Duvalier, what makes you think we're worth this much money?" Ruth wondered.

"Mrs. Whitchurch, I'll be frank … I earned sixty million dollars from my last movie, and that's before you even look at my cut of the merchandising. I'm on for at least the same again with the next one. You're not costing me anything I'll miss."

Alec and Ruth stepped away for a moment to discuss it, though there wasn't, in truth, a great deal to object to.

"We don't work for anyone else," Alec told their host. "I mean, obviously we work for you so long as you're paying, but nobody else. We're our own guys. We don't take orders from Lane Karswell or whatever his name is."

Duvalier shrugged. "No problem. I'll clue everyone in. You'll have the full run of the house and estate, and nobody gives you grief or they're out of here. My word."

More practically, Ruth added: "Also, we've only got an overnight bag. We've no clothes, only a few toiletries …"

Duvalier smiled. "Everything you need will be provided, don't worry. Glad to have you aboard." And he offered his hand.

A few minutes later they'd moved their car into a reserved parking area to the side of the house, and had come back indoors with the little baggage they had. Snow was now falling and settling. The weather man on the radio was predicting a festive freeze for England's western counties.

At the foot of the main staircase, they were met by one of the domestics, a pretty young girl in jeans and sweater. Mike Duvalier clearly ran an informal, and, by the girl's cheery attitude, happy household. She told them she was Sharon and that she'd show them up to their room. From her accent, she was a local lass.

"Doing something for the employment stats, too," Ruth said, grinning at her husband. This was in belated response to a comment he'd made when moving the car that Duvalier was only being generous because he could afford to be.

Alec was about to reply when Ruth saw something that stopped her in her tracks. An arched door at the right of the foot of the staircase gave through to a dining room. This was equally as spacious as the lounge, but not quite so rustic. Its walls were elegantly plastered, and its ceiling corniced in gilt and cream. A little girl was in there, seated at the long Spanish-style table, drawing in a pad with coloured felt pens.

"You go up," Ruth said. "I won't be a minute."

Alec nodded and followed Sharon upstairs.

Ruth sidled into the dining room. The little girl was wearing yellow boots, pale pink snowsuit bottoms, and a t-shirt with Minnie Mouse on it. She was extremely cute: tanned, dark-eyed and pixie-nosed. Her lustrous brown hair was tied in fetching pigtails.

Very casually, Ruth pulled up a chair. "Hi. You must be Claudette."

"I sure am," the child replied, barely glancing up. Despite her Latino looks, her accent was pure California.

"I'm Ruth," Ruth said.

Now the child looked at her properly. "Like Ruth in the Bible?"

"Was there a Ruth in the Bible?"

The child looked shocked. "Aww! You don't know your Bible. That's bad."

"Yeah, you're probably right. Still, I'm a friend of your daddy's. Maybe I can be your friend, too?"

Claudette chewed on a pen. "Are you going to be here for the party tomorrow night?"

"Yes. Your daddy's asked me to stay."

"Are you in the movies?"

"No."

"You should be, you're real pretty."

"Why thank you." Ruth saw that Claudette was drawing what looked like a woman standing in a doorway. "That's a pretty lady too."

"She came to see me yesterday," the child said.

"Is she going to be at the party?"

"I don't know, she didn't talk much. I don't think she's a regular lady."

Ruth almost laughed. "Whatever do you mean?"

Claudette recommenced drawing. "She just watched me. Through my bedroom window."

"Through your …? Sorry honey, what did you say?"

"I was sleepy, so Anita thinks I just dreamed her."

"Anita?"

"My maid. Do you have your own maid?"

"No, I don't."

"Really? Who helps you get your stuff?"

"I have a husband for that. Tell me about this lady."

Claudette chattered on as she drew. "We'd just flown in, so I was real sleepy. Anita says I slept on the plane, but I don't remember. I went to bed as soon as I got here. My bedroom's cool. Do you want to come up and see it?"

"Maybe later. This lady was looking in through the window, you say?"

"I think I dreamed it. Because my bedroom's upstairs and I don't see how she could have got up there."

"And she just watched you?"

"Uh-huh. But then Anita came in and called me a sleepyhead. Said I had to get my body to … adjut, adjut, what's that word?"

" 'Adjust', honey."

"Yeah. I had to get my body to adjust to the new time-zone. Hey, that's the first time I got it right. Is that cool?"

At first Ruth couldn't reply. She was too busy staring down at the picture.

Armed with what she now knew, it depicted a woman not standing in a doorway, but on the outside of a tall, narrow casement. She was clinging on with one hand to either side of the frame. Her clothes were long and flowing, yet even through the child's simple sketch work there was a suggestion of dirt and raggedness. Her facial features seemed normal enough, though the dark hair that framed them was thick and matted and hung down past her waist. It was an odd yet clearly deliberate touch that her eyes had a hint of redness.

6

"Ruth, this is like the biggest load of crap in the history of humanity."

Alec zipped up his fleece and stood shivering in the snow. It was ankle-deep and flakes were falling steadily. They both stared up at the window to Claudette Duvalier's bedroom.

"Are you telling me someone couldn't climb up there?" Ruth said.

The window was some twenty feet up, but ten feet below it a kitchen-annex abutted outward four yards or so. In keeping with the general architecture this too was castellated, but that wouldn't present a major obstacle. To prove her point, Ruth clambered lithely up the drainpipe beside the kitchen window, scrambled over the mock-battlements, and then had only ten feet of sheer wall to scale. That might have been more difficult had it not been densely clad with ivy. She only had to ascend a few feet to prove it would easily hold someone of her weight. She jumped back down and stood next to her husband, beating fragments of leaf from her gloved hands.

"Satisfied?"

"No I'm not," he said. "You're wearing sweats and trainers. We're talking about a woman in a long dress."

"Rags. Not exactly a long dress."

"Okay, you're in peak physical condition. We're talking about a woman who's been dead nearly nine-hundred years."

"I didn't say it was *her*!"

"What *did* you say then?" He started walking back around the house.

Ruth hurried to follow. "Look, I'm only telling you what the kid told me."

"She also told you she thought it was just a dream. Why can't you accept that bit of her story?"

Ruth knew why Alec was in such a huff. He'd accepted this assignment because he'd thought it would be easy, a paid holiday. She, on the other hand, had already set her stall out to do some work, checking all the security rosters, familiarising herself with the staff and their backgrounds. She'd even refused an invitation to dinner that evening with Mike Duvalier, his wife, and those few guests who'd already arrived, saying that she and her husband were now 'on duty'."

"I wouldn't care," Alec complained, as they stamped the snow from their feet in the porch, "but there are security guards all over the estate."

"There's one on the front gate," Ruth corrected him, "and two in the house. Karswell's the head-of-security, remember. He's here, there, and everywhere, checking that his men are doing their jobs. We can't count him."

"Of course we can count him. We can also count the three who are patrolling the grounds. Ruth, every one of these guys has got military training. A couple of them are ex-special forces. This place is locked up tighter than Paddington Green nick. Why don't we just relax and enjoy our good fortune?"

Ruth knew there was no point talking to him when he was in this mood. Alec was a cold-blooded professional, but he was also an ex-cop, and like all cops and ex-cops, he liked to let his hair down once in a while.

"I'm going to take a bath," he said once they'd got back indoors.

He headed upstairs. Ordinarily he'd have preferred a shower, but the bedroom they'd been allocated, which was every inch as large and sumptuous as they'd expected, complete with four-poster bed, tapestried walls and roaring fireplace, had its own en-suite, newly fitted and possessing a sunken marble bath with golden faucets. It was a luxury neither of them had ever experienced before.

Ruth watched him go up. She'd win him around later on in her own inimitable way, but in the meantime she had an interview booked with Anita, who should – Ruth checked her watch – be waiting for her in the kitchen.

Typically for this place, the kitchen was an impressive sight. It was spacious and evidently new, but it had been constructed in the traditional farmhouse style with a brick floor and low, beamed roof. It contained a huge, cast-iron range and worktops of scrubbed pine. Bunches of dried herbs were suspended overhead, while pots, pans and dishes were arrayed on every wall.

Anita, Claudette's maid, was seated at the long central table.

Like the local girls in Duvalier's employ, she affected an informal appearance, wearing jeans and cheesecloth, though clearly she'd come from back home because she was Hispanic. An older woman, she was still very handsome, with dark eyes and long silver-grey hair, which she wore loose. A white-gold crucifix hung at her throat.

"Hi," Ruth said, sitting down opposite. She glanced up and made eye-contact with the cook, a hefty middle-aged woman called Martha, who was the only other domestic present. By prior arrangement, Martha nodded and left the room. Ruth glanced across the table at Anita, who watched her uncertainly.

"Don't look so nervous," Ruth said.

"I don't know what this is about," Anita replied. Her Mexican accent was strong, but, as Ruth had been told, she spoke English fluently.

"It's about Claudette," Ruth replied in the curt but civil tone that she'd always used in interviews. (Never give your own emotional state away – that was the trick).

She opened some paperwork that she'd brought in with her. Anita eyed it warily.

"Now," Ruth said, "you've been with the Duvaliers since they got married, yes?"

The maid nodded.

"And before that you were with Mrs. Duvalier when she was Miss Perdita?"

Again a nod.

"So it's probably fair to say you know Claudette better than anyone does, except her parents?"

This next nod was given with some minor reservation, which Ruth immediately understood. Anita probably considered that she knew Claudette *better* than her parents did, though she wouldn't dare say it.

After this, Ruth got to the point. "This dream Claudette had last night – about the woman at the window?" The maid stiffened. Her face remained blank, but her shoulders went rigid. "What can you tell me about it?"

A taut second passed, and then Anita shrugged. "It was just … just a dream."

"You know that for sure? You checked?"

"Of course. I went straight to the window, I saw no-one."

Ruth sat back. "Did Claudette wake up crying, calling out? Anything like that? Is that what brought you to her?"

"I sleep next door to Claudette. I heard nothing. It was time to wake her up."

"What time would this have been?"

"I would say three o'clock."

Ruth frowned. "In the morning?"

"In the afternoon?"

"Claudette still naps during the day?"

"We just flew in from LA. That's fifteen hours. Then she had a three-hour drive from London. She was tired."

"Of course, silly of me. But let me get this straight, she had this dream while it was still light?" Ruth wasn't sure what answer she was expecting to this, but the idea that someone, if it *had* been someone, had approached the house during daylight was discomforting.

"It was going dark," Anita replied. She shuddered and folded her arms. "It's always dark in this country. The sun doesn't want to rise, and when it does it hurries to set."

Ruth smiled. "That's the Christmas season for you. Don't worry, it lightens up in the spring."

Anita gave a sardonic smile. "In the spring, I hope, we'll be far from here."

"You don't like it much?"

"I have a job. What I think is not important."

"So you don't let your personal feelings get in the way of your work?"

Anita shook her head.

"I know that already, of course," Ruth said, closing up the paperwork. "Or else you'd have mentioned to Mrs. Duvalier about this dream, and I rather think she and Claudette would now be on the next flight home, am I right?"

Anita hesitated before answering. "Family is important. Mr. Duvalier is too long away from his family. I don't wish to make it worse."

"And that's also why you've said nothing to Claudette? I mean about the cannibal woman who's supposed to haunt this house. Clearly you know all about it, Anita. I can tell. Something's frightening you here, isn't it?"

"Does it not frighten you?" the maid wondered.

"I don't believe in it, and neither should you."

Very abruptly, Anita replied: "You lie."

"I'm sorry?"

Anita fixed her with a stare so penetrating that it brought a mild blush to Ruth's cheek.

"When Claudette lies to me, I can always tell. She says 'no' to my question and shakes her head, but her eyes stay fixed on mine. Just like yours did then. That's when I know what she really means is 'yes'."

Amused to have had the body language thing turned around on her, Ruth smiled and stood up to leave, but Anita hadn't finished.

"In my country, we have *La Llorona* … the weeping woman."

Despite herself, Ruth hovered to listen.

Anita explained. "*La Llorona* is a ghastly demon. She haunts the lonely places, wailing for the lives of her children, which she took in a moment of anger. In the villages they say no child is safe when *La Llorona* comes by. She will snatch any little one she finds, and its parents … they never see it again."

Ruth shook her head. "It's like the story here, Anita. It's just a fairy tale."

"Are you a mother?" Anita asked.

"No. No, I'm not."

The maid nodded as if that explained everything. She stood up and left the kitchen. Ruth watched her in silence.

7

They first saw the mistress of the house that evening, when the Duvaliers and a handful of early guests settled for dinner.

Unlike her husband, the female film star looked as impossibly glamorous in real life as she did on the big screen. She was tall and statuesque, as robustly full-figured as only Latin women can be. Her beauty was feline, almost predatory, her silky, raven-black hair hanging braided to waist-length and seeming to shimmer in the low candlelight. In her flowing cream-coloured *Versace* number, low cut at the front and fitted around the body, she outshone all her guests, despite their inclusion of an England footballer and his wife who had both become fashion icons, an upcoming pop princess, and a catwalk model turned chat-show hostess. Even the servants, who, as well as Sharon, included two other local lasses, Lorna and Margaret, had prettied themselves up for the occasion, wearing smart black pinafores with short skirts, dark stockings and high heels.

Yet again it was a glimpse of another world for Ruth and Alec who, thanks to Ruth's decision that they wouldn't be attending dinner, were now relegated to the kitchen, where Martha provided each of them with a plate of game pie, baked potatoes and coleslaw, which admittedly was delicious, as was the bottle of claret they'd also been treated to.

"I spoke to the estate manager earlier on," Alec said.

Ruth looked up across the kitchen table. When the evening had first got underway, they'd mingled for a few minutes in the drawing room, enjoying a cocktail or two. In those brief moments before they withdrew, Ruth had tried to chat with Mrs. Duvalier, whom she'd found distant and uninterested, but had then spotted Alec talking to a short, thickset man with a balding pate, wearing a tweed jacket and green bowtie.

"The slaphead in the dickie-bow?" she asked.

Alec nodded. "Seems there was a fatal accident here a couple of weeks ago. You remember the gamekeeper who filled Mrs. Duvalier's head with all that crap about the child-eating ghoul?"

"Yeah."

"Sounds like he got caught in one of his own traps. A bizarre accident by all accounts, but he died from a broken neck."

"Good Lord. Have they looked into it?"

"Oh yeah, there are no sus circs[3]. He was well past it. Been on the estate since the 1950s. On top of that, he went a bit doolally about twenty years back when someone close to him died. He was kept on this long more out of sympathy than anything else."

"Why was he setting traps?"

"Apparently Mr. Duvalier wants to host shooting parties next summer. He'll be introducing a lot of game birds. This old keeper had taken it on himself to clear out all the potential predators."

"And he ended up breaking his neck?" Ruth was still dubious.

"Seems he'd got himself a couple of bear traps from somewhere."

"Bear traps!"

"Well they don't just go after foxes and weasels, do they? Not anymore."

This was true. Rumours had been rife for years now that big cats were hunting throughout the West Country and along the Welsh border. There was increasing evidence that it was more than just a myth, though to Ruth's knowledge no live specimens had been captured. The feeling among naturalists was that domesticated

---

[3] Police parlance for 'suspicious circumstances'.

leopards and panthers, released into the wild when new 'dangerous animals' legislation was passed in 1976, had turned feral and formed a breeding population. Whether this was true or not, farmers and gamekeepers were increasingly reporting damaged livestock.

"Even so," she said. "Bear traps seem a bit extreme."

Alec shrugged again. "Like I say, he was past it. Just a doddery old fool."

They finished their meals in silence, listening to the gales of laughter and clinking of glasses and cutlery in the dining room. At length Ruth stood up, dabbed her mouth with a napkin, and said she was going to check on Claudette.

Alec put his wineglass down and glanced at his watch. "It's past nine. She'll be in bed now surely?"

"She gets to stay up during the holidays as a special treat."

"You've really got to know her."

"I've spoken to her a couple of times, that's all."

"So why the interest now?"

"She's the reason we're here, isn't she?"

"Where will she be?"

"In her bedroom." Ruth took her dirty dishes to the sink. "Probably playing on her computer, or doing a puzzle. She likes puzzles. Anita does them with her."

"So if Anita's there why do *you* need to be?"

Ruth stared at him. "I'm just doing my job."

"Implying that I'm not?"

"Not sitting around in here drinking wine, you're not."

"Okay." Alec pushed his chair back and stood up. "I'll take a turn around the house. Why not? I mean, there're only six security guards out there already." He handed her his plate and glass. "Just out of interest, how did you find Mrs. Duvalier?"

"A bit cold."

"I saw that. What's the problem, does she not want us here?"

"Dunno. I thought she specifically *did* want us. Maybe she does, but only if we're out of sight and out of mind. Maybe we remind her too much of the problem she's facing."

At which there was a loud burst of laughter from next door.

"You mean the problem that's really bugging her as we speak?" Alec wondered.

"Alternatively, she could just have a lot on her mind."

"Like what?"

"Like being a mum." Ruth strode from the room. "I'd imagine it's quite taxing. But then how would I know?"

8

Ten minutes later Alec was outside, scarfed, jacketed, and blowing on his gloved hands. The snow had stopped falling and the star-spangled sky was clear again, which made it even colder than earlier.

He'd told Ruth that there were six security men outside, but in actual fact that wasn't true. At least one was at the front gate keeping an eye on the paparazzi. Two were inside the house unobtrusively watching the party, and it was anyone's guess where Karswell was. The big security chief had been a bodyguard of Mike Duvalier's for many years now, and was trusted implicitly. He was a former SEAL who knew everything possible about personal protection and home defence. At least once in the past he'd been required to put his life on the line and hadn't been found wanting. But as Ruth had pointed out, Karswell no longer had a watching brief; he now had to monitor all the other guys under his control, and though he was in regular radio contact with each one, he stayed permanently on the move, checking personally that everything was in order.

All of this left a grand total of two men to patrol the grounds. Whereabouts they were Alec didn't know, but for this reason he was more curious than surprised when he saw someone moving across the pristine snow of the football pitch-sized rear lawn. He was on the terrace at the time, a beautiful paved area at the back of the hall, accessible from the dining room via a pair of French windows, which were currently closed and curtained. He watched the dark shape carefully. That was all he could really call it, a 'dark shape'. No limbs were discernible. Neither was any visible walking motion; it was almost gliding over the snow.

Alec strolled to the balustrade. The shape was maybe seventy or eighty yards away. It was moving south to north, but diagonally, a path that would gradually bring it to the main building. "Hello there!" he called.

The figure froze. Then turned stiffly, like a scarecrow on a pivot. Silence followed.

Alec's breath hung in a frosty cloud.

He expected a casual wave from the figure to indicate it was one of the security guys; it would then plod towards the house and meet him on the terrace.

But that didn't happen. Instead, it began to retreat.

Slowly and warily. The way a cat might do having suddenly encountered a dog.

When it turned and fled, it was not back the way it had come but towards the line of trees on the far side of the lawn, and a broad passage leading away through them called the West Wood Walk.

Alec sprinted down a flight of steps onto the lawn, where he found the snow crisp and *very* deep. It plunged past his ankles, and as he was only wearing trainers his feet were soon frozen and soaking wet. He kept going however, hammering in pursuit, scanning the moonlit surface for tracks. Halfway across the lawn, he spotted a churned-up trail. He followed it into the West Wood Walk. The figure came into view again, directly ahead, moving at speed, though how it was managing this Alec couldn't imagine; he was having trouble just keeping his feet. It was a gut-wrenching feeling not being able to call for back-up in situations like this, one he'd never really got used to since going freelance, but his blood was now up.

"I'll get you!" he shouted. "Whoever you are, you might as well give it up now!"

He could still see the figure, though it was a considerable distance ahead. If it reached the rose gardens at the end of the Walk there'd be problems. From what he'd heard, they were laid out in an interlocking mosaic, each one walled off from the next but all accessible to each other via narrow archways. The rose bushes would be dead and snow-laden at this time of year, but there were trellised paths, hidden arbors and all sorts of other hiding places down there, and on the far side of the gardens yet more woods.

Alec ran harder, thankful that he played so much squash. If this person was one of the photographers who'd somehow sneaked into the grounds, he ought to be able to overhaul him pretty soon. But there was no sign of that at present.

Abruptly, the fleeing figure changed direction, darting sideways, vanishing again.

At first Alec thought it had reached the rose gardens, but as he reached the same point himself, he saw that it had diverted from the West Wood Walk fifty yards short of the gardens' entrance. The tracks broke briefly but reappeared on the other side of a low hedge and continued along a less used path, before veering south through a mass of skeletal trees. Alec stayed in pursuit, but it was more difficult here to navigate. The snow carpet was thinner and punctuated with clumps of bracken. And then, at the worst possible moment, the moon vanished into cloud and the snow radiance was blotted out.

Plunged into shadow-filled murk, Alec slid to a halt, panting, lungs aching from the chill air. He stood and listened but heard only the blood thudding in his own ears. For a nerve-racking second it sounded as though heavy footfalls were coming towards him. And then the moon slipped out again, and thirty yards to his right he saw a ruined building.

When he ventured towards it, he did so slowly.

It sat on top of a small hillock and was maybe fifteen feet tall at its apex. It was built from pale stone, but as Alec got closer and saw veins and greenish stains all over it, he realised that this was marble. The building was a folly, or at least that was the impression it gave. It was octagonal in shape, but in each section of wall there was an open entranceway, all equidistant from each other, all upright and perfectly rectangular.

He ascended the hill and when he reached the building, halted warily.

The entrance directly in front of him seemed more like a doorway than the others, which perhaps were merely windows. This one had a lintel, and above that an engraving: a triangle with some kind of astrological symbol in the middle, possibly the Eye of Horus, though it was difficult to tell.

Definitely a folly though.

Alec poked his head inside and sniffed. Compared to the fresh tang of the snowy wood this place smelled damp, mildewed. He hesitated before entering, but the other seven apertures allowed in sufficient moonlight to show that the place was empty, even derelict, so he proceeded. He saw that each one of the other entrances, or windows, had a stump of broken, eroded stonework set into its base. The remnants of statues, he realised, though now that his eyes were attuning to the dimness, he spotted that one of them remained intact. It occupied an aperture on the north side, but though human in outline and roughly Alec's height, none of its features were visible because it was covered with ivy. The same lush undergrowth flowed across the floor to some kind of central grating. Alec glanced overhead. The ceiling, also octagonal and rising to a middle point, was composed of rotted wooden lathes. These had held off most of the snow, though there were gaps here and there through which more ivy hung like lengths of jungle creeper.

There was no guarantee the person he'd been following had come in here, but for some reason he felt it distinctly possible.

He moved first to investigate the remaining statue. The ivy muffled his footfalls, but even so he approached it stealthily. When he reached it, he plucked a few bits of greenery aside, uncovering the marble face of a woman; probably some nymph from the Classical Age, though as her nose had been chipped away and a festering crack bisected her visage, she was no longer the beauty she'd once been. Next, he moved to the grating, which occupied a square aperture in the floor about four feet across.

Kneeling and taking a glove off, he tested the thing with his fingers. Its bars, though thick and heavy, were caked in rust, which meant it probably wouldn't be too difficult to lift. Again, the ivy hung through it in long strands. Alec stood up and replaced his glove. And heard a sound.

In truth he barely heard it.

But it was there – a faint *rustle.*

Directly behind him.

Maybe three feet away.

Alec tensed, balled his fists. Then spun around, ready to go straight into his unarmed combat routine. An intense light speared him in the face, almost blinding him.

"Jesus, it's you," said an American voice. "What the hell are you doing here?"

The hulking shape of Lane Karswell was visible behind the light.

"I could ask the same of you," Alec said. "You aren't the fella I just chased across the rear lawn, are you?"

"No way. I've come from the main gates. You chased someone?"

"I *thought* I did."

"I don't get you."

Now aided by the electric light, Alec gazed around. "I thought he came this way. He was on the West Wood Walk, but then he flitted off through the trees. The next thing I was here."

"I've not seen anyone."

"It's probably nothing …" Alec's words tailed off as he viewed the inside of the building properly. Above and between the apertures, it had been decorated with frescoes depicting mythological figures: satyrs and goddesses in sumptuous garden settings. All were faded and flaking now, streaked with brownish mould. He switched his attention to the grating. "Can you bring your light over here?"

Karswell complied and they peered down. The light penetrated through the bars to a depth of about six feet, where in the middle of a paved floor there was another vent, this one circular and about three feet across. A foot or so down into this the light ran out, but it was sufficient to show aged and descending brickwork.

"Is that a well or something?" Alec asked.

"That's my understanding," Karswell replied, though he seemed more concerned about the alleged interloper. "Who was this guy, do you think?"

"Dunno. Could've been paparazzi."

"Pity you didn't catch him."

"He had a head start."

"If you'd accepted my offer of a radio that might not have mattered."

On first agreeing to join the security team, Alec and Ruth had rejected the offer of personal radios, mainly because they didn't want to be at Karswell's beck and call. Now Alec was wondering if this had been a mistake.

"What is this place anyway?" he asked.

"The boss says it's called 'the Rotunda'. I don't know what it's supposed to be. Apparently it's the oldest part of the property, the only bit left that dates from medieval times."

Alec frowned. "Sorry pal, this isn't medieval."

"That's what I was told."

"Looks more Victorian."

"Whatever, it gives me the God-damn creeps."

Alec nodded. "That we agree on."

9

"Karswell was right," Ruth said. "It *is* medieval."

Alec was standing by the bedroom window watching the huge feather-sized flakes tumbling downward. It would have been richly atmospheric of the season had it not been so ominous. Considering this was only December, it was snowing unusually heavily for the southern half of Britain; it felt as though they were being hemmed in, marooned. Not that this was bothering the dinner guests downstairs, who, by the sounds of it, were having a whale of a time.

He turned to face her. "No chance. That place is definitely *not* medieval."

"No, the Rotunda itself isn't. You're right about that." Ruth was seated at their bedroom desk, a mass of paperwork spread in front of her: recent maps of the estate, deeds, and various other documents she'd requested. "The Rotunda is a folly and it was constructed in 1831. But the well beneath it dates from the twelfth century. It's the only piece of architecture on the entire Killingly Hall estate that remains untouched from the days when Brac Cannor stood on this site."

Alec was surprised. "The castle extended all the way over there?"

"Not the inner section. But the outer wall, the curtain wall, probably encompassed it."

"Do we know any more about it?"

"Yep." She waved a document. "I've got a surveyor's report here. When Mike Duvalier was looking to buy, that well was fully excavated. It's thirty-eight feet deep, but dry and empty. All they found down there was a handful of rabbit bones. It's now Mr. Duvalier's intention to have the well filled in, the Rotunda pulled down and a summer house incorporating a swimming pool built on the spot."

"Sounds like a plan." Alec crossed the room. Ruth's lap-top sat on the desk next to her; its internet link was open, but the in-box empty. She was still waiting on the results of those last-minute questions she'd put to her researchers. "Nothing yet?" he asked.

"Nothing," she confirmed, "and given that it's been Christmas Eve for the last two-and-a-half hours, I'm not expecting anything now until New Year, in which case it'll be no use to us anyway."

He nodded, moved away and started to undress. "You coming to bed?"

"Sure." She folded her paperwork. "But no frisky business. We're going to need all our strength for tomorrow?"

"Why's that?"

"Mike Duvalier, would you believe, has invested in several snowmobiles."

"You're joking?"

"We're all going to have fun and frolics tomorrow, riding hell-for-leather around the estate."

Alec climbed under the covers. "What's the word I'm looking for again? Oh yeah, *hooray*."

Ruth chuckled. "You sound like Claudette. She doesn't want to do it either. She'd rather go ice skating."

"Ice skating. Where?"

"On the ornamental lake over in the east spinney. It's a lake in name only. But it's still forty feet deep in the middle."

"I hope you kicked that idea in touch for her."

"I did and she went to bed sulking. Apparently, she's been snowmobiling in Vermont, and it's boring."

Alec lay back. "These kids, eh? I don't think I'd even seen a snowmobile when I was her age. I don't think I've seen a proper one now, if you want the truth."

10

The following morning, Alec finally *did* get to see a snowmobile, and he was impressed.

There were seven of them, and they sat in a neat row on the rear lawn, which by nine-thirty was a useful ten or eleven inches deep. They were all from different manufacturers – Yamaha, Polaris, Arctic Cat – and in different styles. But they were beautiful creations, larger and more powerful looking than either of the private investigators had expected, with sleek streamlined bodywork, plush saddles, broad runners at the front and glinting steel 'rip-saw' tracks at the rear. They were designed for hardened sledders of course, extreme sportsmen and women, and as such were painted in action colours: black and scarlet, blue and silver, venom-green, ember-orange. Jags of lightning adorned their hoods and exhausts; their headlamps were fitted close under the steering-bars and slanted outward like demonic eyes. When Mike Duvalier started one up, its four-cylinder engine rumbled like a primeval beast.

There was even a customised junior model for Claudette: a smaller version of the others, painted pink and white as if to match her snowsuit. Yet the child was still unmoved. She was carrying a varnished wooden box with a shoulder-strap and told Ruth in quiet confidence: "I've got my skates in case it gets colder."

"This is old England, honey, not New England," Ruth replied. "It hardly ever gets colder than this."

The child looked dropped-on. "Does that mean I still can't skate?"

"I'm afraid so. Over here the winter freeze doesn't last long enough to make the ice on our rivers and lakes very safe."

"I tell her this but she doesn't listen," Anita put in tartly. "She says *you* know this country better than me."

The maid looked and sounded peevish that morning, and Ruth thought she knew why. The previous evening she'd gone up to visit the child's bedroom and Claudette had ignored Anita from that moment on, preferring to make puzzles and play computer games with "mommy and daddy's new friend".

For some perverse reason of her own, Ruth felt no need to apologise for stepping on Anita's toes in this way, and a few minutes later, though she'd come outdoors clad for winter sports, the maid disappeared inside again.

As there weren't enough snowmobiles for everyone, it was agreed that some would either have to share or miss out. However, the footballer and his wife were determined to have one each, Claudette and the pop princess both wanted one, and it seemed out of the question to expect either the host or hostess not to partake in the fun. So that left one sled to be shared between Alec, Ruth and the chat-show queen. The latter announced that it was too cold for her anyway. She'd rather relax in front of the fire and sip mulled wine while Sharon, Margaret and Lorna decked the house for the coming party, so she vanished indoors. At Claudette's urging, Alec said he wasn't bothered about snowmobiling either and, in truth, he wasn't. He was just pleased to have woken up that morning and found a brand-new set of outdoor clothes awaiting him: a thick plaid shirt, a Goretex jacket, and a heavy Parka with a fur-trimmed hood, plus a pair of hard-wearing ice boots. As the outfit given to Ruth was a silvery, figure-hugging ski-suit, she looked somewhat better than he did, though neither could compare with Mrs. Duvalier, who as always was the star of the show in a gleaming white ski-suit, complemented by an overcoat of flowing white fox-fur.

Considering the actress hailed from a sunbaked land and had lived most of her adult life in southern California, she handled her sled with practiced ease. It was impossible not to admire the graceful way she looped and turned across the snowy lawns.

"Who does she think she is," Ruth said to Alec, "Lara bloody Croft?"

"Shouldn't you be wearing a crash helmet or something?"

"No-one else is."

"Just be careful, all right."

She kissed him on the cheek, then pulled down her yellow-tinted goggles, fixed her bob-cap, and accelerated away after the others. Initially she swerved from side to side, looking certain to capsize, but then regained control of the machine and throttled up, skimming off over the cream-smooth surface.

It was an ideal day for it. The snow was deep and powdery, the sky a pearlescent blue. The partygoers whooped, hooted and bellowed as they scooted back and forth. Along the edges of the lawn, security men in their uniform black coats, black scarves and black gloves, watched quietly. Everything seemed to be in order, and at length Alec retreated to the terrace, from where Karswell surveyed the whole scene through a pair of binoculars.

"We had another snowfall last night," the chief bodyguard said.

“I noticed.”

“It’s obliterated all trace of those tracks that led to the Rotunda.”

Alec nodded. “I thought it would. Listen … is this snowmobile thing entirely safe?”

Karswell pursed his lips. “As professional bodyguards, we can protect these VIPs from just about anything, Mr. Whitchurch. Except themselves.”

*

Ruth wasn’t finding her machine as difficult to handle as she’d expected, though the speed of the wild, uncoordinated game was a little hair-raising. The pop princess was keeping nervously out of everyone else’s way, but the footballer and his wife were proving to be deft hands, which was probably no surprise. No-one, however, was having as much fun as the Duvaliers themselves. They were right in the thick of it, spurting snow everywhere as they rode reckless rings around each other. But it was about ten minutes in when Ruth noticed the absence of Claudette’s pink and white ensemble. The child had proved as adept a sledder as any of the adults, a testimony to the long vacations she’d spent in Vermont and other luxury winter resorts. But there was no sign of her now.

Ruth swung out of the main scrum and pulled a long, slow circle around the outside as she craned her neck to look. The child had definitely gone. Ruth glanced towards the house. Alec and Karswell were standing by the balustrade on the terrace. Neither seemed alarmed or agitated, but that didn’t necessarily mean everything was all right. Claudette’s machine wasn’t parked up there, so she hadn’t just opted out of the game and gone indoors.

And then Ruth spotted her tracks: they veered away from the main action in an easterly direction, crossing an otherwise unblemished stretch of snow before disappearing through an arched gateway. Ruth knew what this meant; even on that icy morning, a new kind of chill went through her. She sped off in the same direction. Two minutes later, her worst fears were confirmed. She crested a low hill to find the ornamental lake spread in front of her. Claudette had abandoned her snowmobile on its west side and was now a diminutive figure on the glazed surface, at least forty yards from shore as she glided on her skates.

Ruth braked sharply, leaped from her machine, yanked off her goggles and raced to the water's edge. It was immediately obvious that the ice wasn't safe. It was semi-translucent rather than white, and bubbles were sliding around underneath it. The air temperature was well below zero, but it had only been this low for a couple of days.

Not nearly long enough.

Claudette noticed her and waved casually.

"Hi honey," Ruth called. "I thought we agreed this wasn't a very good idea?"

Claudette didn't reply at first but when she did, she sounded sulky. "I'm bored on my buggy."

"If you're bored, how about the two of us build a snowman or something? That could be cool, don't you think?"

"I always build snowmen. They're boring too."

"Okay, what about an ice palace? I used to be a whizz at building those."

Claudette glanced up. "An ice palace?"

"Yeah, just like the sort of thing you see at Disney World, only made from ice."

"Don't you need a big ice block for that?"

"In England we use snow, but you compact it hard enough and then smooth it off, and when the next big freeze comes, hey presto, it's turned to ice."

Claudette pondered this as she slid closer, but then swerved away again. "That sounds like fun, but I want to skate first." She didn't notice the surface crack that suddenly shot across the lake from one side to the other. Partway along it, a subsidiary crack branched off.

"Honey, I don't want you to skate, okay!" Ruth was trying hard not to sound panicky. "It's too dangerous."

"It isn't dangerous."

Ruth bit her lip. What was she to do? How did you balance the carrot and stick in a situation like this? How would a real parent deal with it?

"I thought we were friends," she called.

"We *are* friends."

"But you're not listening to me."

"Sure I am." Claudette turned a graceful spiral. "But that doesn't mean I have to do what you say. You don't have to do what friends say."

"But I'm a grown-up friend, and that means I know more stuff. And I honestly and truly think it would be a good thing now if you stopped and went to the side."

"Claudette began speed-skating. "You do?"

"I wouldn't be stopping your fun unless there was a really good reason, would I?"

"I guess not." Slowly, reluctantly, Claudette came to a halt. She was still fifty yards away, but probably only fifteen from the farther shore.

"Go on now," Ruth encouraged her. "Just for me."

"Okay. But only this once. If mom says it's all right, I'm going skating again, and we can do the ice palace later."

Claudette made to come back across the centre of the lake, but Ruth held up a warning hand. "Not this way, honey. Go to the other side. I'll meet you round there."

Claudette looked puzzled and vaguely rebellious again. But then, in the way of all youngsters who've decided the complexities of adult thinking can't be fathomed, she nodded, spun around and headed the other way. Ruth watched anxiously, expecting the pink and white-clad form to drop from view at any moment as a section of ice overturned. But nothing happened. Claudette made it ashore and stomped awkwardly up onto firm ground. She bent down to unfasten her skates, and that was when Ruth spied the second serious threat of the morning.

Behind the child, a tall, thick privet hedge ran north to south, breaking once for a slatted gate. There was a narrow gap at the hedge's base, only the thin privet trunks visible in it, so Ruth could see through to the other side – where what looked like long skirts, torn and raddled with filth, dragged swiftly along in the direction of the gate.

The breath caught in her throat.

She didn't wait to see more but jumped onto her snowmobile and swung it around in a tight circle before revving away along the waterline. Straight across the lake, it was probably sixty yards tops; but following the perimeter it was more like two-hundred, and it wasn't a straightforward ride. On this south shore, trees came down almost to the water's edge, so Ruth had to veer through and around them. There were also stones and small boulders, and worst of all, gnarled roots elbowing up through thc snow.

It was one of these that undid her.

She had thirty yards to go, her focus fixed on the gate, which Claudette had somehow contrived to get even closer to as she struggled with her remaining skate. And then Ruth's entire world overturned.

There was a deafening *CLUNG* of steel.

The front of her sled rose like a plane taking off, but at a sideways angle.

The next thing she knew she was turning over in mid-air. She released her grip and fell bodily away from the saddle. But it was too late.

The snowy ground rushed up at shocking speed.

She never even felt the impact.

*

All Ruth would later remember about the accident was waking up facedown, the snow like a freezing hand clamping her nose and mouth. Coughing, gasping for breath, she rolled onto her back, and found herself gazing at a blue winter sky through a network of leafless boughs. Only slowly did she recall what she was doing here, and that was mainly due to the conversation she could hear taking place somewhere nearby.

It sounded like a little girl, an American kid, talking with someone who might have been an adult, though that second voice was oddly indistinguishable.

"Really?" the child said. "That would be cool. Can we go now?"

Ruth tried to sit up but went dizzy. Hot fluid trickled into the hollow of her left eye; when she blinked it left a crimson blur. A pounding headache was commencing.

But none of that mattered.

She was on duty, she remembered. She was here to protect.

"Claudette!" she blurted, scrambling to her feet.

Again, she went groggy, and had to lean on a tree. She glanced to her right. The snowmobile lay upended. It didn't appear damaged, but its engine had cut out. She looked further afield, trying to work out exactly which way was which. The ice sheet on the lake lay to her left. That meant she had to go forward … didn't it?

She stumbled drunkenly in that direction. Even under the trees, the snow was deep. It tugged at her ankles, but slowly her strength was returning.

"Claudette!" she called again, staggering around the southeast corner of the lake. She could see the child's abandoned ice-skates. "Claudette!"

The voices were still conversing, but on the other side of the hedge. Ruth ran panting up the slope towards the open gateway, shouting again as she blundered out through it.

She found herself in a narrow lane. Again, it was picture perfect, like something from a Christmas card: long and straight, deep in glistening snow, with frosted evergreen shrubbery on either side.

Claudette was there, but alone. For a moment her pretty little face looked cross.

"There!" she said. "You frightened her away."

"Who?" Ruth asked, turning to look down the stretch of lane behind. There was no sign of anyone that way either.

"The lady. The one who came to see me the other night. *Ohhh!*" The child's voice softened. "You've hurt yourself."

"I'm okay," Ruth said, producing a handkerchief. She dabbed at the cut on her upper left brow. "Who is this lady, Claudette?"

"I don't know who she is, but she's real kind. She wants to show me where she lives."

"Is that what she said to you?"

"Something like that. She spoke strange. She's real pretty though."

"She is?"

Claudette smiled fondly. "She's got this lovely long hair, like it's been growing forever."

Ruth was about to reply, but others were approaching. Whether someone had heard the impact of the crash or, just by chance, had happened to come looking for the missing pair wasn't clear, but snowmobiles growled to a halt on the far side of the hedge. Mike Duvalier came through the gate first, followed by Alec.

"Everything okay?" the actor asked, a look of genuine concern on his pink-tinged face. He spotted Ruth's injury. "Jesus H. Christ!"

Alec hurried over to check it out. "What the hell happened?"

Ruth moved away from him, took Claudette by the hand and turned to face the pair of them. "We need to talk. *Now.*"

11

It was mid-afternoon at Killingly Hall, and the 'Christmassing' of the mansion was in full swing. Holly sparkled along the shelves and mantels, mistletoe hung in every doorway, and swags of meshed conifer twigs adorned the banisters. A gigantic spruce fir had been erected next to the main stairway, and Lorna and Margaret were up on ladders, festooning it with tasteful ornaments. The kitchen was a chaos of French caterers, who'd arrived to take care of that night's festive food. Guests were due to arrive from early evening onward, but the conflab that had begun just after lunch in the billiards room was still in progress. It consisted of Ruth, Alec, Mike Duvalier, and Lane Karswell, and despite the crackling hearth and mugs of mulled wine that had been given to everyone to warm them up after their outdoor exertions, the atmosphere was solemn.

Ruth, who now wore a strip of Elastoplast on her cut, was in full flow. She'd stood up and was going over everything that had so far happened, adding in the various tidbits of information that she'd collated concerning the long, eerie history of the house.

"Everything," she concluded, "points to there being something about this place that isn't quite right."

"Don't you think maybe that whack on the head was a bit much for you?" Alec wondered.

She glared at him.

"Mrs. Whitchurch," Duvalier said from his chair. "You're not actually telling us you believe this story? I mean about the undead baroness?"

"No," she replied. "But that doesn't mean there isn't some lunatic around here who does. I suppose it's been pretty well publicised that you were buying this place?"

"Well, yeah."

"There you go then. I mean come on, you and your family must have to deal with stalkers all the time. Surely none of this is surprising you?"

Duvalier rubbed his chin. "The fact we've got someone following us isn't the issue. It's the way you say they're doing it: dressing up in a Halloween suit to try and scare us?"

"Mr. Duvalier, I think it may be a bit more serious than trying to scare you. This woman, whoever she was, attempted to lure Claudette away."

"What exactly did she say to her?"

Ruth shrugged. “It’s difficult to know for sure. You and your wife speak to Claudette by all means, but interviewing youngsters can be tricky. They tend to tell you what they think you want to hear. Either that or they clam up depending on how much trouble they decide it’s going to land them in.”

Duvalier frowned. “What I’d really like to know is how she got onto the estate in the first place.” He turned and stared at Karswell, who was busy knocking balls around the table. “You told me everything was a hundred percent secure.”

Karswell straightened up awkwardly, but it was Ruth who answered for him. “Mr. Duvalier, there’s no way anything can be a hundred percent secure, particularly not a country estate of this size.” She glanced at Karswell. “Some of its perimeters probably aren’t even walled, are they?”

He made a vague gesture. “There’re a couple like that, but they’re fenced. We’ve got security cameras up, alarm wires …”

“But suppose she was already on the site before you put that rig in place?” Ruth asked.

Alec intervened again. “Ruth, love … we don’t even know for sure that it *is* a ‘she’.”

“It isn’t just Claudette’s testimony we’re relying on,” she said. “I heard a voice, myself. You’ve all seen this drawing.” She picked up Claudette’s sketch of the figure at the window.

“You’re not suggesting it’s a guy in drag, I hope?” Duvalier asked Alec.

“No, he’s suggesting it’s no-one at all,” Ruth said.

Duvalier looked surprised. “Your wife’s also your business partner, but you don’t trust her judgment?”

Alec half-smiled. "Of course I trust her. It's just that …"

"What?"

"Nothing."

There was a brief silence, during which Ruth wondered what Alec's problem was. She knew he'd come here hoping for a paid holiday, but it was unlike him not to respond to what was clearly a crisis. It was also unlike him not to have faith in her. When she'd been sergeant to him in the Met, long before they'd got together, he'd always said she had the best instincts of any detective he'd worked with.

"So what do you suggest?" Duvalier asked.

"We keep a much closer watch on Claudette," Ruth said. "Confine her to the house, certainly for tonight and tomorrow."

"No can do. We're taking her to the local Catholic church tomorrow for the Christmas Morning service. Rosa's insisting on it."

"I'm sure that'll be all right," Alec put in.

"Be certain there's someone with her at all times," Ruth said. "And I don't just mean Anita."

"What's wrong with Anita?" Duvalier asked.

"Is she any good at self defence? Does she do martial arts?"

"No," he admitted. "But she can carry a gun. In fact, we all can." He turned to Karswell. "You might as well break out the weapons …"

"Whoa, whoa!" Alec interrupted. "What do you mean 'weapons'?"

Duvalier stood up. "I paid you guys to find out whether or not there was a genuine threat to my daughter while she was here. You appear to have given your expert opinion, and that's good enough for me." He addressed Karswell again. "Get the guys in, we're arming them."

"Arming them?" Alec said. "You mean with firearms?"

"I don't think sticks would count for much."

"Mr. Duvalier, you do this and you won't be able to call in the real police."

"And if we call the real police how many men do you think they'll spare us, given that our chief suspect's a cannibal woman from the Middle Ages?"

"Look, maybe it's difficult for an American to understand … but you just *can't* do this!"

"Who's going to stop me?"

"You think it'll go unnoticed?"

Karswell halted by the door. "We're not going to be walking around brandishing AK47s, if that's what's bugging you."

Alec shook his head. "You can't walk around brandishing anything. This is England. Security guards don't carry guns here."

"Your country's pretty proud of its tough firearms regulations, isn't it?" Duvalier said.

"Yes. And so it should be, if you don't mind me saying."

"I don't mind you saying at all. But where do you think I got these weapons from?" Duvalier watched the ex-cop carefully. "Put it this way, I didn't smuggle them in … I'm not that much of a dumbass. But I had a feeling we'd need to pack at some point, so I had Lane make a few enquiries."

"I'd like to know where," Alec said.

Karswell chuckled. "I'll bet you would."

Duvalier also moved to the door. "Something you probably don't realise, Mr. Whitchurch – money can buy you virtually anything. Even in law-abiding England, which as you showed me when you first got here, isn't quite as law-abiding as everyone thinks."

The door closed as he and Karswell left the room.

Alec shook his head. "Bloody great. I came here expecting *Holiday Inn* and we've finished up with *Reservoir Dogs*."

Ruth was less disturbed by it. "We carried when we were on the job. Regularly."

"We were professionals."

"For God's sake, these guys are professionals." She re-gathered her paperwork. "Lord knows, Alec, you were quick enough to say that to me when I expressed concern that the place wasn't secure enough. But you know what … they *could* be carrying AK47s and I'd still not be satisfied." She also made for the door, but not before adding: "You want the truth? I'm genuinely worried there's something here that's way beyond our experience."

"You know that's crap …"

"And your attitude isn't helping. At the moment, Alec, we're half a team, and that would be no use even against run-of-the-mill opposition."

The door banged closed behind her.

Alec gazed at it uneasily. He knew that his wife had been badly affected by her second miscarriage, particularly as it had resulted in her needing a hysterectomy. He'd hoped, however, that several years down the line the psychological effects of that would mostly be past. But throughout their stay at Killingly Hall he'd watched her grow increasingly protective towards Claudette. Okay, *that* was their brief – to protect the child. But from the outset, Ruth had seemed determined to do more than that, becoming unnecessarily friendly with the kid, developing an emotional tie, which was strictly *not* in the rulebook. This was possibly a result of Claudette's real mother's apparent coldness. The woman had barely spoken to Alec and Ruth – which was probably understandable, as she'd regard them as hired help – but she also seemed a distant presence where her daughter was concerned, preferring to party with her guests. This was at odds with the story they'd heard about how worried she was for the child's safety, and it was difficult to rationalise. It must be especially difficult for someone like Ruth, who yearned to have children of her own and never would have.

Alec considered his options. Tackling his wife on this subject would not help. What could he do, tell her to buck up and stop moping? With Ruth's fighting spirit, that could have exactly the opposite effect of the one desired. Even suggesting discreetly that she was overreacting might fall on stony ground; she'd simply reply that she was doing her job to the best of her ability. Which left one avenue only: taking issue with the *irrational* streak she was showing, the bit about the evil baroness. In the real world of crime and crime-fighting, which the two of them had occupied for so long together, there was no room for fantasy, and in her heart of hearts she'd know that. He was certain that when all this was over, she'd assess the way she'd behaved and perhaps be a little embarrassed. In which case it was time to nip things in the bud.

He hurried up to their bedroom. Ruth was seated in front of her laptop, reading through several emails.

"Ruth," he began, "I appreciate this assignment is proving tougher than we expected. But tell me one thing, at least. You don't seriously believe that we're dealing with some kind of monster here?"

She said nothing, continuing to read.

"Ruth?"

"I hear you." She sat back. "Take a look at this."

It seemed that her research people had delivered after all. They'd provided three items in particular. The first was extremely short. It was an excerpt from a modern translation of an original medieval document charting the fortunes of the Villehardoin family, Norman nobility, several of whom – as Ruth and Alec had already become aware – had accompanied William the Conqueror on his invasion of England. The cover letter sent by the researcher explained how the branch of the Villehardoins that settled in England died out less than a century later, when, according to the text:

Ralph, the only son of Earl Gilbert, fell prey to a demoness ...

In the typical style of a medieval chronicle, the compilers of which would know their intended audience were already familiar with the historical events they were referring to, this was the sum total of it. Tantalising though it was, nothing else was offered.

Nevertheless, Ruth was triumphant. "That's the second allusion we've found to the guy who took over this place in the twelfth century losing his kid in ultra-weird circumstances. And this one was written at the time."

Alec shook his head. "This is so much bollocks."

"Well, look at this next one."

The second item dated from a much later period and had been found in an obscure tome detailing the personal writings of Oliver Cromwell. It comprised two letters, both written by Cromwell himself after his crushing victory over the Royalists at the battle of Worcester in 1651. The first one instructed his able lieutenant, Charles Fleetwood, to take a detachment of troops and travel to

... the manse called Killing Lea, whereupon fire and steel be employed to cleanse that region of its horrid spectre.

"Remember that entry in the guidebook?" Ruth said. "Cromwellian troops destroyed what was left of the medieval castle. Now we know why."

Again, Alec shook his head. "The 'spectre' he's talking about could have been the spectre of Royalism."

"Oh yeah? Read on."

The second letter was more extensively quoted. It was again addressed to Fleetwood and in it, Cromwell offered congratulations for a successful mission but also expressed regret at the events that had necessitated it. It contained the following passage:

There is no more tragic thing on God's green Earth than the loss of infant life. To hear of so many plucked like catkins while still in the blossom of youth can rend the hardest heart. Thou didst the Lord's work this day.

Alec pursed his lips. All the evidence she'd so far turned up, this included, was circumstantial. However, he had to admit that it was now turning into something a little more convincing. Still he opted to play devil's advocate. "He's probably referring to war casualties."

"Get real, Alec!" Ruth pointed at the screen. "These are Oliver Cromwell's own words. Remember everything you were taught about him at school? He was a fanatic, a zealot. He'd have fought that civil war on his own if he hadn't had support. I very much doubt his heart was rent at the thought of any collaterals who might've got in the way."

"What's the third one?"

"Well …" She smiled. "That's the clincher." She called up the third and final document, stood aside and allowed him to read.

It was an extract from a diary, that of Mrs. Mabel Farrington, the wife of a well-to-do farmer. According to the accompanying notes, again courtesy of the researcher, the diary offered little more in general than a mildly diverting account of eighteenth century rural life, and was of such little historical significance that it had now been relegated to the 'forgotten' shelf. However, during Mabel Farrington's life she had been friendly with the Hart family of Killingly Hall, who'd either been her neighbours or her landlords.

On the date of May 15th 1799, she'd recorded the following entry:

Today we buried Mr. Selwyn Joseph Hart, a broken man since fire engulfed his home six months ago. Mr. Joseph now lies with his late lamented wife in the churchyard at Hinton. After services, a most pleasant knife and fork tea was provided, but frivolities must not distract from the sadness of this matter.

Losing his wife, though she was never, as I knew her, in good health, was a great calamity. But the loss of his two young children hurt Mr. Joseph deeply in those final years. Often afterwards, his servants reported him running around the grounds of his residence at night, his hair unfixed, calling out challenges to that mythical fiend.

When last we spoke, he cursed himself for his blindness. He said that, had he believed the gruesome tale handed down, his children would still be alive. Many years ago, his own brother, he claimed, disappeared from the same part of the estate whilst playing with a hobby horse. Mr. Joseph himself had dreams as a child in which a frightening figure tapped on his bedroom window. These he later dismissed, being as he always asserted, "a man of Enlightenment".

How he came to regret this Enlightenment. How he rebelled against it.

Whispers in the county hold that he personally struck the flame that took away his home. Grief had overcome his senses, and with nothing left in this world, he sought an all-consuming revenge.

All well and good, but if past tales are aught to go by, I fear the horrendous thing that so tormented him has not yet departed. Last week in the village, we buried a wooden doll in place of the milkmaid, Susan Barnabus, ten years old next June and now missed for a whole month ...

"We already knew fire destroyed the hall that was built during the age of Wren," Ruth said when Alec had finished reading. "Remember the 'delectable edifice'? Again, now I think we know why."

"This woman's just surmising."

"This woman is better informed than we apparently are. She alludes to all sorts of facts that we haven't even got close to."

"Facts?"

"What about the second fire?" Ruth asked. "The one in 1837. Was that an accident, or did something similar happen then too?"

"Okay, all right." Alec had to admit to feeling slightly unnerved by the new data. "I'm prepared to accept that kids have been getting kidnapped around here in recent times, maybe even murdered, and that it's somehow slipped under the intelligence net. But trying to connect it with these earlier cases is ludicrous. There's hundreds of years difference."

"That doesn't conflict with *my* hypothesis," she replied.

"Come on Ruth, you don't really believe in this! Maybe you were right before. Someone knows the history, and they're copycatting. It happens."

Before they could argue further, there was a knock on the bedroom door. Alec told whoever it was to enter, and Karswell appeared. He closed the door behind him, before dumping a military-type haversack on the floor, reaching in and taking out two leather armpit holsters, the grip of a handgun protruding from each one.

"Mr. Duvalier's orders," he said. "There's a piece here for each of you, if you want it."

Ruth had no hesitation. She took one of the harnesses and slipped out a Glock 20. She held it up to the light. It looked to be in good condition.

"You know how to handle that?" Karswell asked.

She laughed. "Don't worry. Got any spare clips?"

He fished a couple out of the haversack and handed them over, before looking at Alec. "Mr. Whitchurch?"

Alec stood with hands-in-pockets, before finally shrugging. "Hey, why not? No point being the only sane man in the asylum."

When Karswell had left, Alec watched his wife sit down at the bureau, push her laptop aside and expertly take the handgun apart. Satisfied, she snapped it all back together and slid the clip into place.

"You know," he said, "if this enemy we're facing is what you think it is, that gun isn't going to do you any good."

"And if it's what *you* think it is, it will," she replied. "So where's the problem?"

"The problem is that it could get us a mandatory five years for possessing unlicensed firearms."

"A risk I'm willing to take. Sorry, Alec, but they don't call this place the Killing Ground for nothing. I feel better strapped."

12

"It's spot-the-celeb down there," Alec said, coming back into the bedroom.

He'd just been downstairs, which was now crowded with guests all dressed as per the Dickensian theme, though he himself looked less than comfortable in his maroon tailcoat, high collar, large red bowtie and tight white pantaloons.

"How do I look?" he asked.

"Like Bob Cratchit," Ruth replied.

He swore under his breath.

His was one of two costumes that had been brought up to them earlier, Sharon having taken their measurements first thing that morning and then rushed off to hire something. Ruth was in front of the mirror, putting the final touches to her own outfit, a beautiful off-the-shoulder ballroom gown of white silk. It had a full flounced skirt and a close-fitting bodice, though underneath that she'd been required to wear a whalebone corset and knee-length knickers (in her case, it seemed that Victorian garb also meant Victorian underwear). To complete the picture, she'd put on a pair of white net mittens and had tricked her hair into blonde ringlets, dressing it with trimmings of white feathers, which thankfully covered the plaster on her temple. She finished off her makeup and slipped the Glock 20 into a dainty white purse.

"Sure the safety's on?" Alec asked.

She gave him a withering look before checking that his own weapon was in place – concealed under his tailcoat and then they went downstairs together.

It looked as if quite an evening lay ahead. Mike Duvalier was resplendent in a Germanic military uniform made from peppermint-green satin, with stripes of gold braid across its chest and gold tassels at its shoulders. At his left hip was a real cavalry sabre, and under his right arm a bearskin with a green plume. Many of his guests had opted for similar Victorian-inspired fantasies, so as well as the run-of-the-mill shawled ladies and top-hatted gents, there were also Ali Babas, Sinbads, Fagins, Pickwicks, Alices, Heathcliffs, Robinson Crusoes, and numerous other figures from pantomime or popular fiction. And as Alec had said, quite a number of these were recognisable as celebrities: at least two other American movie actors were present, along with a famous director, the presenter of a TV cinema review show, several British soap stars, a cabaret singer, a bestselling authoress, and of course an abundance of hangers-on.

It was now eight o'clock and the evening was in full swing. Three musicians, a fiddler, a trumpeter and a drummer, provided a riotous succession of Christmas tunes. In the main drawing room, traditional parlour games – Blind Man's Buff, Snapdragon, The Minister's Cat – were in progress, while in the dining room an astonishing smogasbord of seasonal goodies was on offer. At one end of the table: caviar sandwiches, devilled oysters, creamed sweetbreads, cold, boned turkey, ham and mustard, and duck with apple stuffing. At the other end: leek and salmon pie, quails and eggs, rabbit in red wine, 'pigs in blankets'[4], roast beef, roast goose, roast pheasant, lobster salad, and ribs in sticky sauce. For dessert there was almond cake, plum pudding, gingerbread, candy canes, marshmallows and chocolate; the list went on, and none of it less than mouth-watering.

Here to work, Ruth and Alec split up and began to mingle, though in such an atmosphere it was difficult keeping their mind on the job, especially when they were constantly being offered drinks (everything from *julmust*[5], to eggnog). In the midst of it all, Ruth spotted Claudette dressed like a sugarplum fairy and running back and forth, delighting the guests as she darted between the legs of the Hapsburgian-clad waiters who'd been hired to assist Sharon, Lorna and Margaret. Anita, who, in a nod to her position, wore a starched and rather severe governess costume, was never far from the child. The security men were all there too, watchful but keeping well out of the way.

And still the guests continued to arrive.

Outside, flaming torches had been placed to either side of the drive all the way from the gates to the front of the house, and a stately cavalcade of expensive cars and horse-drawn carriages were progressing up it. The fact that stray snowflakes continued to fall only elevated the mood more, though perhaps the first real highlight of the

---

[4] UK slang for chipolata sausages.

[5] A sweet Christmas beer from Sweden.

evening came at 8.30, when the lady of the manor finally deigned to descend.

There was much clapping and whistling as Rosa Duvalier made her well-rehearsed entrance, coming down the stairs slowly and in grand fashion, which was probably essential as her extravagant 'snow queen' costume was large and complex. A figure-hugging white dress which suited her statuesque form admirably, was overlaid by a huge cloak of what looked distinctly like layers of polar bear fur and swan's feathers. Needless to say, she was dripping with jewelry, much of it white-gold, and was made up to a silvery sheen, her lip gloss and eye shadow sparkling as though tinged with frost. Her hair hung in glittering raven coils, and above that her head-dress was the sort of thing the White Witch in the Narnia stories might have worn: a tall crown made from what appeared to be upright shards of glinting ice.

The audience *ooohed* and *aaahed* ecstatically until she'd reached the bottom of the staircase, where her proud husband was waiting, forearm extended. Then, together, the party hosts went to meet their guests properly.

Ruth couldn't help thinking what a pity it was that Mrs. Duvalier's penchant for the theatrical wasn't matched by her acting ability, or her singing talent for that matter. Still, Rosanna Perdita had appeared in a number of movies that were box office smashes and had released several hit records, so what did Ruth know? She glanced around to check where Alec was and spied him on the far side of the drawing room, chatting up, or being chatted up by, the pop princess. Probably it was the latter. Ruth had laughed at him for looking like Bob Cratchit, but in actual fact he didn't. With his square jaw, bright eyes and strong, even features, he was more like

Steerforth from *David Copperfield* or Brooke from *Tom Brown's School Days*. Damn, but she had a handsome spouse. She knew Alec felt the same about her, but she was more critical when it came to herself; Ruth hadn't felt like a complete woman for several years now.

Not that she didn't have to fend off a couple of toothy predators during the course of the party. Earlier in the evening, it was the England football star who wouldn't take 'no' for an answer, but then his wife had come down from wherever she'd been getting ready and glared at him. There was also a politician present, a rather loutish member of the Cabinet, who always made a big issue of his northern accent and terse manner, presumably because he thought it made him a character. In recent times he'd fallen from grace, and now Ruth could see why. From the constant innuendos he whispered to her, she could only assume there was truth in the current scandal that this married man, who'd never ceased to fire sleaze allegations at the Opposition, had supposedly tried to seduce a parliamentary secretary. With the self-confidence born of giving orders and shouting down junior colleagues, this political specimen was even harder to shake off than the henpecked footballer; eventually Ruth had to have a quite word in his ear, telling him that she was with the security team and, slipping briefly into a stronger-than-usual version of her own Yorkshire accent, advising him to "bugger off" or else lose his "no doubt minuscule meat and two veg".

A variety of entertainments followed. There were several formal dances, a thespian to provide recitations, and then a party of mummers clad from head to foot in evergreens, who performed various Yuletide escapades. The main treat of the evening was to be the arrival of Father Christmas, but he was not due until midnight, and this caused dismay to Claudette, who had to be in bed by ten.

"But I want to see Santa," she said as Anita tried to lead her upstairs.

Ruth leaned down to console her. "Honey, I'll tell you a secret. It isn't the real Santa, it's someone dressed up."

Claudette looked even more distraught. "You don't believe in Santa?"

"Sure I do. But this isn't him. This is just someone coming to the party pretending to be him. The real Santa will only come and see you when you're asleep."

"Even here? Suppose he doesn't know where I am?"

"He always knows where you are."

"I still want to see him."

"Well, maybe you will." Ruth brushed a crumb of mince pie from the lapel of the child's costume. "Just pretend to be asleep – but either way you have to be in bed."

"Will you come up with me?"

"Of course."

Ruth took one diminutive hand and Anita the other, and they started up the stairs together, the child pleasant and chatty again.

"So, who's looking after your babies tonight?" Claudette asked Ruth.

"Oh, we don't have any babies."

"Awww! I bet that means Santa's never been to your house, huh?"

Ruth was silent for a moment, then said: "Not since I was little, myself, no."

13

When Ruth eventually came downstairs, she found Alec standing by the roaring hearth, sampling a snifter of champagne and enjoying the attentions of two busty blonde cuties, who'd arrived in the company of a famous but these days rather skuzzy nightclub owner.

She drew him to one side. "I hope you're not enjoying this party too much."

"Ruth, chill out. Nothing's going to happen. Look, apart from Karswell's guys, half the guests have got bodyguards here too. You seen the drive? There's a line of fellas next to the cars who look like they're auditioning to be the next Bond villain. Only someone too stupid to understand the meaning of the word 'danger' would try anything on a night like this."

"Or someone to whom the word 'danger' has no meaning at all," she replied.

He watched her thoughtfully. "How's the kid?"

"Settled in her room. In her bunny rabbit pyjamas, playing on her computer."

"I thought she'd been sent to bed?"

"She's got a half-hour stay, then she has to hit the sack."

"Is the bedroom door locked?"

"No. Apparently there's no en suite in there, and she may need to go to the bathroom. But Anita's with her and Karswell's right outside. He's got a chair and he's staying there all night."

"In that case we can relax a bit." Alec stopped a passing footman, placed his empty glass on the tray and took two fresh ones from it. He handed one to Ruth. "Here. It's Christmas Eve, after all. We ought to make a little time for each other. On that subject, I have a confession to make. Since we've been here, I haven't really had time to get you anything."

"What do you mean?"

"You know, a present."

Ruth looked baffled that the issue had even arisen. She shook her head slowly. "There's nothing you can get me that I want, Alec. There's nothing anyone can get me."

"I know, I just ..."

She put her drink on the nearest table, untouched. "Let's keep our mind on the job. The night's still young."

She made a tour of the premises, checking all entrances. Despite the cold outside, a couple of the windows downstairs had been left open for ventilation purposes. Ruth ensured they were fixed on the narrowest gaps possible, then went to the front of the house and looked down the drive. As Alec had said, it was crowded with chauffeurs and security men. Trays of food and drink had been taken out to them, and many were socialising loudly rather than keeping watch, but there was still a feeling of strength in their numbers.

She heard Alec's words again as she went back through the house: "Nothing's going to happen." She had to admit, it looked unlikely. On the upstairs landing she checked that Karswell was still outside Claudette's bedroom. He too was in Victorian dress but stripped down to his waistcoat and shirtsleeves. He was seated on a chair next to the door, his greatcoat over his knee to conceal his drawn firearm. Satisfied, Ruth moved along the passage to a window, and gazed out to the rear of the property. It was a serene vista: the sky had cleared again, the moon a silver jewel suspended over the Welsh mountains. In the immediate foreground, the snow lay in a flawless blanket. Lights from the house were streaked across it, reaching as far as the trees, which were heavy and still, every branch laden with white. There was no movement.

She went back down to the party, feeling better. But then, at quarter to midnight, Father Christmas arrived, and her worries reignited.

In keeping with the party's theme, Mike Duvalier had opted to hire a Victorian Father Christmas; an old druidic figure, the traditional spirit of winter as immortalised by Dickens in the Ghost of Christmas Present, rather than the jolly, elf-like character made popular by Coca Cola in the early twentieth century. As such, he wore a green cloak rather than a crimson one, and though this was still trimmed with white fur, his beard and moustache were red. Rather than a hood, he had a mass of straggling red hair, and on top of this a holly wreath thick with scarlet berries. Of course, there were some similarities to the modern caricature. He was of big, ungainly build, he entered 'ho-ho-hoing' and stamping snow-covered boots, and he had a huge sack on his back bulging with presents. By the looks of them, these were the special edition DVDs that Duvalier had been autographing the previous day, all now gift-wrapped.

However, of all the Father Christmases Ruth had ever seen – and some of them had been pretty odious (bored pensioners in cheap department stores, drunks in fancy dress fighting in town centres) – there was something especially sinister about this one. In particular his face, or rather his lack of face. The dense red beard was attached to a papier-mâché mask. Whoever had made this, had tried their best to fulfill the Christmas fantasy: the fat, apple-red cheeks; the large, bent nose; the bushy eyebrows; the broad, grinning mouth. But putting all these together, there was something about it that wasn't quite right.

Possibly the eyes.

These were holes through which the person beneath could look, but to Ruth they were empty sockets, menacing slits with only darkness behind them.

The first thing the star turn did, once he'd entered the room to a fanfare of clapping and cheering from the sozzled crowd, was dance. The three musicians went straight into a frenetic rendition of *Santa Claus is Coming to Town*, and he capered wildly back and forth. Other Christmas jigs followed, and he continued to dance, but now amongst the guests, handing out a present to each one. Ruth watched him and the way he moved. For a big man he was rather nimble, she thought. In fact, 'nimble' wasn't the word; nor was 'lithe', nor 'agile'. There was something practiced and effeminate about his mincing and pirouetting.

She sidled over to Alec. "Who is this guy?" she whispered.

"Who, Santa?"

"Who else?"

"Dunno. Some dancer Duvalier hired, apparently."

"Doesn't he seem a little light on his feet?"

Alec glanced sidelong at her. "They usually are."

"No, I mean … well, for want of a better word, doesn't he seem a little *girlie*?"

"Like I say, they usually are."

"I wish you'd take this seriously!"

"What exactly are you driving at?"

"Goddamn it, Alec!" she hissed. "There's a woman under there."

"So?"

"What do you mean 'so'?" Ruth's face flushed. "It's the one way that hag could've got in here! Think about it … Duvalier hires a dancer. We don't know who he is. We don't know how he got here, or where he parked his car, or whether or not he came in through the front or round the back through a tradesman's entrance. But one thing we definitely *do* know: he won't have had a minder with him."

"Why would he need a minder, Ruth?"

"To protect him from ambush."

Alec took his wife by the elbow and led her to a corner, away from where two curious guests had started earwigging. "Ruth, I am seriously getting worried about you."

She pulled her arm loose. "Humour me, just for a minute."

He nodded but was clearly becoming exasperated.

"She lies in wait …" Ruth began.

"Who does?"

"Lady Morgana."

"Oh yeah, how stupid of me. The woman who's been dead nine-hundred years."

"She lies in wait," Ruth reiterated, "she takes him out, she puts his cozzie on, and wham-slam she's inside the house without anyone realising."

"Okay, she lies in wait for him," Alec said. "Just one problem with that – how the hell did she even know he was coming?"

"She just knows. That's the way it is, she's a predator …"

"She doesn't exist, for God's sake! Ruth, you've got to get a grip!"

Ruth glared past him to where the Father Christmas figure, its sack emptied, now performed a courtly bow in front of the Duvaliers. "I'll get a grip on *her*. Look over there … are you telling me that's not a woman?"

"What are you suggesting we do, pull our guns on Father Christmas? We'd go down in history with the bastard who shot Bambi's mum!"

"We watch, all right?" she said fiercely. "We watch!"

But watching was easier said than done.

A couple of minutes later, Ruth glanced up and saw Claudette's face poking through the spindles near the top of the staircase. She hurried up there and found the child in pyjamas and dressing-gown, sitting gazing down at the party.

"What are you doing here, honey?"

At first, the child was too excited by what she was witnessing below to respond.

"Claudette?"

"Is that him?" she whispered. "Is that Santa?"

"No, that's someone just pretending to be. You're supposed to be in bed."

Claudette shook her head. "I've gotta pee-pee."

Ruth took her hand. "Well, you can't do that here. Come on to the bathroom."

At the top of the stairs, Karswell was waiting, hands in pockets.

"What the hell are you playing at?" Ruth demanded.

He looked shocked. "There's no harm in letting her have a peek. It *is* Christmas."

Ruth was about to say something else, but now remembered that it *was* Christmas, the most exhilarating night of the year for young children, and that if she continued to overreact like this, she might just spoil it.

"Claudette needs to pay a visit," she said. "Where's Anita?"

"In the armchair. Aslccp."

"Great."

"You know, she only flew in a few days ago. She's not a young woman, and she's jet-lagged to the eyeballs."

Again, Ruth realised that she was crashing around like a bull in a China shop. She took Claudette to the bathroom, herself, and then marched her back to the bedroom, now dim with low-key lamplight. Anita was indeed asleep in the armchair, so Ruth put Claudette to bed and tucked her in. Mischievously, the child felt at the red, gold-trimmed stocking hung alongside her pillow, feigning disappointment that it was still empty.

"You'd better go to sleep now," Ruth advised. "Don't keep the real Santa waiting."

"I might need to pee-pee again."

"How much lemonade did you drink?"

"Enough to fill our swimming pool in Bel-Air."

Ruth folded the coverlet back, to make the child more comfortable. "That must be some house you've got."

"That's only one of them."

"I imagine it is." She kissed Claudette on the forehead. "Come on, night-night."

The child rolled over and closed her eyes in a determined effort to get to sleep. Ruth turned to leave. Before she did, she glanced at the window. The curtains were partly open, and visible on the other side of the pane were feathery striations of a type that as a child she'd believed to be the handprints of Jack Frost. She wondered fleetingly if they might on this occasion be the handprints of someone else.

Karswell was hovering about on the landing, but he'd now put his scarf and greatcoat back on. His costume was new and in good condition but owing to his face and build, it made him look less like a Victorian gentleman and more like Bill Sikes. He even wore his topper at a rakish, villainous angle.

"You off somewhere?" Ruth asked, closing the bedroom door.

"Got to check the rest of the guys. I'll be five minutes. Can you hold the fort here?"

"Yeah, sure."

Karswell moved away. Ruth sat down and glanced at her watch. It was close to one o'clock. She didn't know how long these celebrity parties lasted. At a guess, well into the early hours under normal circumstances; but of course, this was not a normal occasion and the host and hostess had a young child with whom they wanted to share Christmas morning. She felt at the concealed plaster on her temple. As she grew more tired, the ache increased. Perhaps she could try to snaffle some painkillers from somewhere. She stifled a yawn – and then jumped bolt-upright.

Someone had just screamed downstairs.

And it had been a *real* scream; gutsy, loud, filled with terror.

It was all Ruth could do not to snatch the pistol from her purse. She hurried downstairs, where the music had come to a halt amid a confusion of shouts and squeals.

The drawing room was in bedlam. Someone had switched the main lights on, and the majority of the guests were crowded into one particular corner. There were mutters of concern and exclamations of disbelief, but someone was also sniggering.

Ruth fought her way through the throng. "Excuse me!" she said testily. "Excuse me!"

But when she got to the middle, she discovered that it was a minor incident. The pop princess, much the worse for drink, had apparently been dancing on a tabletop when the table had collapsed. Now the young diva lay spread-eagled in the midst of broken bottles and overturned plates, her voluminous petticoats so disarrayed that she was displaying stocking-tops, suspender straps and in terms of actual underwear, a very unladylike nothing at all.

"Don't waste your time, love," the footballer's wife told the girl scathingly, as she helped her to her feet. "No paparazzi have been allowed in here."

"Someone check her thighs aren't injured!" a drunken voice shouted. It sounded like the cabinet minister. "If it's one of the fellas, lucky you. If it's one of the lasses, can I watch?"

Laughter sounded, followed by more unkind quips, but the pop princess was in too much of a daze to comprehend, and in any case the bulk of those gathered were eager to get on with the party. The lights were lowered again, and the music resumed.

Ruth turned to find Karswell standing behind her, eyes bulging.

"You going back upstairs now?" she asked him.

"Er, yeah. Okay." He lumbered off.

She turned again, looking for Father Christmas, but now, rather disconcertingly, was unable to locate him. Eventually she fixed on Alec, standing near the Christmas tree and eating chocolate truffles from a paper dish.

"How about that," he said as she came over. "Free food, free booze and a strip-show chucked in."

"Where's Santa?" she asked.

He looked puzzled. "Weren't you supposed to be watching him?"

"You were supposed to be watching him too!"

"Relax, I was. All he was doing was giving out presents. Then he went through to the kitchen to get something to eat. Sharon took him."

Ruth also went through to the kitchen, where Sharon, Lorna and Margaret stood tittering together.

"Hi," Ruth said. "Where's Santa?"

The girls, who had now removed their maids' aprons and hats and were helping themselves to a bottle of sherry, continued to giggle at some joke.

"Er … he's not here now," Sharon said.

"I can see that."

"He's gone looking for Claudette," Margaret put in.

"Looking for Claudette," Ruth replied, cold. "I thought you guys were feeding him?"

Sharon nodded at an untouched plate of food on the table. "We've made something up for him, but apparently there's a special present he wants to give Claudette first."

All Ruth could think about as she dashed from the kitchen, along the passage, through the dining room and then up the main staircase, was how long she'd left Claudette's bedroom unguarded during the distraction caused by the pop princess. Karswell had gone back up there two or three minutes ago, but that still left several minutes unaccounted for. Skirts to her knees, Ruth reached the top of the stairs in record time. She made a beeline for the child's bedroom door, which stood open. There was no sign of Karswell.

She barged into the room.

And that was where she found him.

He lay face-up on the bed. His mouth had been forced open, and a mass of holly protruded from it. Clearly this was only one end of a hefty bough, because his cheeks and throat bulged unnaturally; in some places the flesh had split and tiny green tips were visible. Specks of congealing blood were dotted around his lips. His eyes, wide and horror-filled, were slowly glazing over.

Ruth stood for a second, too stunned to move.

Aside from Karswell, the bed was empty. As was Anita's armchair. But now Ruth could sense movement. Just behind her.

She spun around, Glock already drawn.

The wardrobe door had come ajar, apparently of its own accord. A narrow gap showed only darkness inside, but Ruth *knew* there was a presence in there. She'd been out of the police a few years, but she hadn't lost her instincts yet. She cocked the gun, pointing it with both hands and gazing along its barrel.

"Okay, I know you're there," she said. "Out now, where I can see you!"

There was no response.

"I'm armed and I want you out of there, *now!*"

A low moan followed; it bespoke grief and deep anguish.

Ruth cursed and yanked the door open. Anita was curled in a ball at the bottom of the wardrobe. Hanks of hair hung over her face, and her eyes were red with weeping. She clasped a Catholic rosary to her breast, working her way through it bead by bead.

"*La Llorona*," she sobbed, "*La Llorona …*"

14

Initially, Ruth was almost completely overcome with panic. The temptation was to scream and shout for help, but again her 'inner cop' kicked in. She turned and surveyed the room, and spotting the curtains billowing, rushed over there.

The central panel of the window was wide open, a quick inspection showing that it had been forced from the other side. And now something else caught her eye:

movement down below. She leaned out to look. A projecting buttress of the building blanked out the majority of the terrace, which was some thirty yards to her right, but there was still sufficient of it visible for her to see two figures there. One was clearly Claudette; the child was only in her pyjamas, dressing-gown and a pair of dinosaur feet slippers, but even though she was standing in snow, she seemed happy. She clapped her hands with glee as the other figure, the green-clad shape of Father Christmas, cavorted around her in a circle. He still had his sack with him, empty by the look of it, though he was gripping it in both hands, holding it open as though he intended to use it; either to fish out one last present or, more likely, to stuff something inside it. Before Ruth knew what she was doing, she was out through the window. Balanced precariously on its snow-covered ledge, she peered down the twenty-foot drop. As she'd proved to Alec before, it was scaleable – in either direction.

Though not in this dress.

She reached behind her, yanked the zip down and let the whole thing rustle to her knees before stepping out of it. It would have given the lecherous cabinet minister quite a turn to see her like this: corset, bloomers, white stockings, white leather ankle-boots.

She took the Glock between her teeth and scrambled down the ivy.

Huge portions of it came away in her hands, but she made it safely to the roof of the kitchen-annex. From there, she swung over the parapet, hung by her arms and dropped. Fleetingly, as she rolled in the snow, Claudette was out of her sight again. Ruth shouted hoarsely as she got to her feet and started running. As she staggered up the steps to the terrace, she pointed the gun in the air and fired two warning shots, which were deafening in the frosty night. When she got up there, both Father Christmas and Claudette were staring in her direction. Claudette looked incredulous to see the state Ruth was in, and even more so to see the gun, which was trained firmly on her jolly mentor. Father Christmas's expression, hidden beneath his papier-mâché façade, was more inscrutable.

"Drop the sack," Ruth panted. "*Drop it now!*"

The festive figure opened his hands and the sack fell harmlessly to the ground.

"Ruth?" Claudette pleaded. She sounded tearful, and why not? It was Christmas Eve, and she'd finally met Santa, and now this had happened.

"Honey, I know this is confusing for you, but just move away from him and stand near the balustrade, okay?" Ruth said.

Claudette hesitated.

"Please do it, honey. You know I wouldn't ask unless it was very important."

More than a little reluctantly, the child plodded through the snow towards the balustrade, leaving Father Christmas alone, watching his captor wordlessly.

"Okay … you," Ruth said, "get that damn mask off now."

He raised his green-gloved hands.

"Slowly," Ruth added. "Very slowly."

Beyond the French windows, the music had ceased and she could hear voices raised in consternation. They'd probably heard the shots and would now be searching for the source. Good; that meant help was on its way.

The suspect's hands hovered at either side of his head.

"Okay," she said. "Let's see who you really are."

Slowly, he lifted the mask, which wasn't easy because apparently it was attached to the whole of his head-dress. From the corner of her eye, Ruth saw the curtains open behind the windows, figures framed against the firelight. She was even more pleased; let everyone else now see what she'd already guessed.

"*Get it off!*" she shouted.

He finally complied, to reveal – as Ruth had suspected – that *he* was in fact a *she*. Even so, it was a complete surprise to see the face of quite a young girl, seventeen years old at the most. She had frightened, rabbit-like eyes, from which mascara had trickled down onto her flushed cheeks, probably through a combination of sweat and tears. Her rosebud lips clamped tightly together.

Wonderingly, Ruth lowered her weapon. "Who the hell are you?"

The girl released a catch, and her heavily padded costume fell away, revealing a slim figure wearing a leotard and tights.

"Tilly Cordwell," she said in a small voice. "I run a dance class in the village."

"What were you doing with Claudette?" Ruth demanded.

The dancer shook her head. "I … I've got a present for her in the sack, a special one. I was searching for her, but during the commotion when that girl fell off the table, Claudette sneaked out of her bedroom and came downstairs. In the chaos, no one saw her come out here. Apart from me. She says she was looking for my sleigh."

"So … you haven't been upstairs?"

"No."

There was no point questioning Tilly Cordwell further. From her nervous body language, it was obvious she was telling the truth. Ruth swung towards Claudette, not knowing whether to admonish her for disobeying orders or to apologise for spoiling her big night – just in time to see a flutter of pink dressing-gown as the child vanished over the balustrade.

"Claudette!"

Ruth raced to get over there but slipped and fell in the snow. She leapt back up and stumbled the remaining fifteen yards. The balustrade stood four feet tall, which meant the child could not have fallen backward over it, though in truth there was no question of Claudette having fallen. She'd clearly been dragged. One of her dinosaur feet was now lying on the terrace. The other lay eight feet below on the snow-covered lawn.

Once again, Ruth flung herself over a parapet, hung by the arms and dropped. This time, she went over on one of her ankles. The pain was excruciating, but she clambered to her feet and limped forward.

"Claudette!" she cried.

There was no response. No movement was visible on any side, though the snow was disturbed in a wide area; a crafty trick to disguise retreating tracks. But even if it hadn't been like that, any tracks would have been difficult to follow with only moonlight to illuminate them.

"Claudette," Ruth whimpered.

Then light flooded over her. It was harsh, intensely bright, and the throbbing growl of a small but powerful engine accompanied it. Ruth backed away. She pointed the gun.

"Planning to take me out as well as Santa?" Alec asked.

He'd slid to a halt, mounted on one of the snowmobiles.

“Claudette’s been snatched,” she stammered. “And I don’t know where she’s been taken.”

“I do,” he replied. “Hop on.”

She climbed on behind him. “You sure you know how to control this thing?”

“I can’t do any worse than you this morning, can I?”

He revved the machine to life, and it leapt forward, careering sideways under the unaccustomed weight, before righting itself and shooting away across the snow.

“Karswell’s dead,” Ruth shouted over his shoulder.

“I know, I’ve just seen his body.”

“Who could do that to a bloke like him?”

“Someone extraordinary, I’d say. Someone who’s lived nine centuries maybe and is still going strong.”

“Oh … so you believe me now?”

He swerved onto the West Wood Walk. “I dunno. Difficult to see I’ve any choice.”

“Where are we going, anyway?”

“The Rotunda.”

“Why?”

“Because it makes sense. If your theory’s correct, that well underneath it is the only part of the property that dates from the time when this woman actually lived here. It’s the only thing left she can truly call home.”

“She lives in a well?”

“Nasty thought, eh?”

They veered off the Walk and wove dangerously through the belt of trees, encroaching quickly on the lone outpost that was the Rotunda. Travelling at such speed, it was difficult to see whether or not they were following fresh tracks, but Alec was in no doubt. As soon as they skidded to a halt, he dismounted, ripped off his tailcoat and drew the Glock from his armpit-holster. As an afterthought, he offered the coat to Ruth. She pulled it on gratefully, but then said: “Wait a minute, just wait – this place has been excavated, remember? All they found down that well were rabbit bones.”

“Maybe they weren’t rabbit bones,” he replied.

And with that cheerful thought, he indicated they should split up, signalling that he would approach the building from the east while she should circle around to the south.

They advanced uphill, guns levelled. Whoever was hiding in here – if someone *was* – they’d definitely have heard them arrive. But in both Alec and Ruth’s experience, dividing your force and catching the enemy in a crossfire was always preferable to bunching and making an all-in-one target of yourselves.

Not that on this occasion there was any immediate resistance.

They entered the Rotunda simultaneously, Alec through its main entrance, Ruth through one of the window apertures. As before, the octagonal interior was an empty shell, a void of darkness crosscut by beams of glacial moonlight. However, their eyes attuned quickly, and they saw that the heavy grating covering the well had been raised on its hinges and now was in the upright position. They halted, ears pricked. Alec glanced once more around the interior. Aside from the grating, it was exactly as he’d left it the day before yesterday, dank and musty. The sole remaining statue still occupied its aperture, the classical silhouette made ugly by the shroud of ivy that hung over it.

They advanced again, reaching the grating and peeking down. Six feet below, the frail shape of Claudette lay motionless on the paving stones at the very edge of the circular well; one of her arms hung down into it.

Ruth shoved the Glock into her coat pocket and made to climb down.

Alec grabbed her shoulder. "Hang fire! You don't think this is a trap?"

"She only needs to roll over and she'll fall thirty-eight feet!"

Alec glanced around uneasily. "I don't like it."

"You've got my back, haven't you?"

"Yeah, but …" There was obviously no alternative. "Okay, go on."

Ruth swung over the edge, but he held her by the wrist as she descended, just to ensure she didn't drop into the well herself. A moment later she was on her knees beside the child.

"Claudette?" she whispered. "Claudette?" She felt for vital signs. "There's a pulse, thank God."

"Get her up here, quick."

"I don't know where she's hurt yet. It might not be safe to move her."

"For Christ's sake, Ruth, we can't leave her down there."

"Just give me a sec."

She checked underneath the child's body with gently probing fingertips, mainly paying attention to the spine and skull. Above, Alec looked nervously around again. A chill breeze whipped across him, hissing through the snow-laden woods outside. There was still no movement, though he started when he spotted what he thought was someone lying full-length against the foot of the wall opposite. When he looked more closely, he recognised it as a remnant of one of the other statues.

He glanced back down. "How you doing?"

"She's absolutely frozen. She could be in hypothermic shock, I don't know."

"All the more reason to get a move on."

Alec felt increasingly tense. He couldn't believe that after all the trouble this thing had gone to, it would just abandon the child where they could reach her.

A shadow passed one of the upright apertures.

He raised his gun.

It could've been anything, he told himself: there were animals all over this part of the country. It could be Karswell or one of his guys. But no, it couldn't be Karswell. Karswell was dead. The import of that struck Alec like a gut-punch. Lane Karswell, a former SEAL, was actually dead; he'd been brutally murdered.

"Hurry up, Ruth," he said tightly.

"Gimme a second."

"We might not have a second."

He glanced across the interior again. Had another shadow just flicked past? No, it hadn't, as it probably hadn't before. The silver moonlight and tangled branches outside were creating optical illusions. But where was this damn woman? Why didn't she attack? And then a different thought struck him.

Alec turned stiffly, gazing to where the broken statue lay alongside the wall. Now that he came to think of it, there hadn't been a statue lying there before; at least, none that he'd noticed. Hardly daring to breathe, he edged towards it. Even from two or three feet away, he could clearly see that it was marble. Its surface was cold and white; a jagged stump showed where it had been broken from its plinth.

Yet it had *not* been here the last time; of this he was certain.

Another thought now struck him – an outrageous one.

He turned again, rounding on the statue still standing in the aperture. Was it his imagination, or did it look slightly taller than previously? He approached until he was standing only a foot away. The last time here, he'd torn the ivy off to expose its face. That face now was hidden in shadow, its features indiscernible. Alec leaned forward slowly until they were almost nose to nose.

It opened its eyes.

They were fiery red, their pupils tiny black beads.

"Shit," he breathed.

It struck him, lashing out from the ivy it had hidden beneath. The blow caught him in the chest, and sent him staggering backward, but not before he was able to point his Glock and get off three quick shots, all of which he was sure were dead on target, yet none of which appeared to have any impact.

The thing sprang out from under its cowl of foliage.

Alec saw a tall, misshapen form clad in the rags of old robes, its limbs wrapped individually with aged, mummy-like bandaging. He managed to regain his balance just inches before toppling backward into the well. And then they were facing each other again.

Long, ratty hair hung past the thing's ember eyes. A new smell filled the air: dampness, mildew. It came at him. Alec dodged to one side, but it moved with such speed that it blurred in the moonlight. He squeezed off one more shot – again he was sure it was dead-centre – before a twisted claw sent the gun flying from his grasp. Alec threw a punch, but his wrist was caught and a savage impact landed in his midriff. The wind *whooshed* out of him. A third blow followed, this with an open hand – if it could be called a hand – raking him across the face, laying his cheek open. He'd have been flung to the floor like a broken doll had his assailant not still got a grip on his arm. She – it, whatever, whoever it was – swung him around with frightful force, releasing him and sending him cartwheeling until he crashed bodily into a wall and fell senseless into the ivy.

Ruth was now standing up, but several inches lower than the rim of the grating hatch, she couldn't see what was happening. As the tall shape glided past overhead, it grabbed the grating and slammed it closed. Ruth's first response was to half-duck. Her second was to jam her Glock up through the bars.

"Stay where you are!" she shouted. "Stop or I'll fire."

It didn't stop, so she fired: three shots before the angle became impossible.

Like Alec, Ruth was certain she'd hit the mark – to no visible effect.

Alec meanwhile, dazed, was crawling on his belly along the footing of the wall. He could sense the figure approaching from behind, could smell it again. He got up and tried to run but was too groggy and fell. He heard a noise like a scraping of stone. Fuddled, he craned his neck around to look.

The monstrosity had hefted something up and over its head.

The statue of the nymph.

It was made from marble but was life-size. It had to be prodigiously heavy, and yet the thing held it high as it advanced, arms ramrod straight. It was going to crush him, flatten him like a beetle.

"Lady Morgana?" Ruth's voice sounded from beneath the iron grating. But she spoke gently now, beseechingly. "Lady Morgana … please don't take my husband from me the way yours was taken from you."

A terrible second followed. The crimson blots of the thing's eyes burned down through its strands of raddled hair as it towered over Alec, and yet it seemed to hesitate.

“I can’t imagine how terrible the suffering they put you through, or how awful the pact that entraps your soul,” Ruth added. “But I can guess. I was never blessed with a child, though I’ve always wanted to be. You *were* blessed, but then you lost him. Doesn’t that make us alike? Aren’t we sisters? And if so, would you punish your sister as cruelly as *you* were punished?”

Alec lay rigid, peering up. Still, no real detail of the horror’s face was distinguishable, though he now realised that its ragged, patched-up clothing was the source of the stink. The thing had no smell of its own. It wasn’t even breathing. On a night when living breath hung in opaque clouds, none at all issued from this being.

Yet it was listening.

“Those you’ve already taken will understand,” Ruth pleaded. “They’ll forgive you, I’m sure, if you’ll only make an effort to fight back. In life, you were your husband’s shield-maiden; you fought to the last for what you believed in. Remember that heroism, that courage? Show it now, I beg you. Break this chain of events, lift the curse that’s held you here. Spare another being those pains *you* suffered. Lady Morgana, return a husband to his wife, but, above all, return a child to its mother …”

Her words petered out. The thing made no effort to lower the stone, but likewise it made no effort to throw it on top of Alec.

And then, *BANG!*

The gun-flash was shocking in its brightness.

BANG! BANG! Two more shots followed, glaring white, their detonations thunderous.

With each one, the tall figure jerked violently, finally dropping the statue to one side.

BANG, a fourth shot. It tottered backward.

BANG, a fifth. It lurched towards the nearest wall, but *BANG*, a sixth, and it was hurled from its feet, dropping into a writhing, agonised heap.

The air was suddenly rank with an acrid stench of gunpowder, and Alec found himself gazing in bewilderment as Rosa Duvalier stepped in through the Rotunda entrance. Her coat of white fox-fur billowed majestically around her. In one hand, she clutched a long barrelled revolver, a six-shooter, something reminiscent of the Old West. Its muzzle still smoked.

"Poot-ah!" she hissed, her beautiful face written with cat-like malice. "Back to hell, bitch!"

15

Even as Alec watched, the figure on the floor stopped moving, and appeared to slowly collapse, to sink in on itself. There was a groan of disbelief, and Alec realised that other figures were congregated at various of the building's apertures, and by the sounds of it, more were arriving.

He climbed shakily to his feet.

Rosa Duvalier, meanwhile, had crossed the Rotunda, and was attempting to lift the iron grating. It budged, but only slightly. Alec joined her, along with another man – Mike Duvalier himself who, rather ludicrously, had his sabre drawn.

With a torturous squeal, the grid was raised.

"She's okay," Ruth said, as she handed the unconscious child up to them; Claudette was pale-faced, but wrapped in Alec's jacket as well as her own dressing-gown. "I've checked her out, I can't find any injuries. But she needs a doctor. I think she's in shock."

Rosa Duvalier said nothing, just took the child in her arms and, crooning into her ear, rushed away, exiting the building.

"Goddamn!" Mike Duvalier said.

He prodded his sword at what a few moments earlier had been the body of Alec's assailant. The steel tip found only dust and cinders. He sank it in, stirred it around, overturned it in clumps. Eventually he kicked at it with his boot; it broke apart, and a couple of bent bullets rolled out to lie glinting in the moonlight. Slowly, the dust began drifting in the strengthening breeze.

"I never thought it'd work," the actor muttered, sounding stunned. He glanced around at Alec, who was helping Ruth up through the hatchway. "Those damn bullets."

"Bullets?" Alec asked, distracted.

"These." Duvalier pointed. "Another condition of Rosa's before she agreed to come here. I had them specially made. Six silver bullets, melted down from six crucifixes and blessed in the cathedral by the Bishop of Santa Cruz. I thought anything for a quiet life, but I really didn't expect it to work. Hey, you guys okay?"

Ruth sat on the edge of the hole. In her dirtied underwear she looked bedraggled and weary and, by the way she was huddled, extremely cold. Alec, who was bloodied and bruised, but on his feet, grunted that they were all right.

"You guys are amazing," Duvalier said. "Totally amazing. You want to stick with me, you've got jobs for life."

"Security?" Alec asked.

"You bet. Specifically for Claudette. I've seen how close you've got to her, particularly *you*, Mrs.

Whitchurch. After these last few days, I can't think of any person I'd trust more to protect her."

Ruth glanced up at him. "I can. Her mum."

"Rosa? She's not home all the time. She's still working."

"She was here when she needed to be, wasn't she?" Ruth said. "She took the action that needed to be taken. I didn't."

"Come on, love …" Alec said, but Ruth shook her head as she climbed to her feet.

"I could never work for you again, Mr. Duvalier," she said. "Because I'd feel I was conning you. In fact, if you want my opinion, we should refund you everything you've paid us so far."

Duvalier glanced from husband to wife. "I don't get it."

"Neither do I," Alec said.

"We failed," Ruth explained. "Or rather, *I* failed."

At that point, Duvalier was called from outside. It sounded like Rosa's voice.

"Look, I've got to go." He sheathed his sword and moved to the entrance. "We're taking Claudette straight to ER. You guys go back to the house. Get yourselves warmed up. Take a hot bath, anything, the place is yours."

And then he was gone. Along with most of his guests, who hurried to keep up with him. In less than a minute, the two private eyes were alone.

"Ruth," Alec said, "just because you didn't happen to have a gun that worked on her …"

"It's nothing to do with the gun. Or the bullets. Or blessings in cathedrals."

"How can you know that?"

“I just know, Alec. I do. Because it’s something far more miraculous than any of that.”

She clamped her mouth shut and shrugged, as though none of this had really bothered her. But tears leaked onto her cheeks, and finally she leaned against her husband. He put his arm around her as he steered her outside, where they discovered that someone had pinched their snowmobile. It seemed a small price to pay for having survived, but it was still a long trudge back to the house.

Behind them in the Rotunda, the remaining dust blew in swirls around the dark, empty hole.

SOURCES

The Christmas Toys was first published in *The Screaming Book of Horror*, 2012.
Midnight Service was first published online on *Killer Reads* (the HarperCollins blog), 2012.
The Faerie was first published in *Traps*, 2008.
The Mummers was first published in *Shadows and Silence*, 2000.
Thc Killing Ground was first published in *Ghost Reulm*, 2008.

Printed in Great Britain
by Amazon

48902098R00124